Solitude Showdown

A Jim Taylor and Buck Novel

Lee R. Atterbury

Printed in the United States of America by Lightning Source, Inc.

Published by BookCrafters, 2012.
Joe and Jan McDaniel SAN-859-6352
http://self-publish-your-book.com
bookcrafters@comcast.net

ISBN 978-1-937862-14-5

Library of Congress Control Number: 2012905257

Cover design by David Bahm
Cover photo credit istockphoto.com
Author photo by Alexander S. Kammer

Copies of Solitude Showdown may be ordered from
www.bookcrafters.net and many online bookstores.

To Sally

For never letting me quit

Chapter 1

Even squinting he couldn't see beyond the horse's head. He trusted Buck's night vision, the darkness impenetrable to his human eyes. He could feel the downward slope of the trail and imagined he was descending into the bowels of the mountains. It was quiet under the trees, the forest seemed to absorb all sound, even the animals' hoof beats were muffled. The quiet added to the sense that he was inside some organism.

A chill breeze came from behind bringing with it a sharp, clean whiff of pine sap and an eye watering blast of ripe mule. The horse grunted.

"Pfff," he exhaled, "I'm with you on that, old friend." He yanked on the lead rope to keep the mule on course and flexed his fingers to get the blood moving, hoping for a little warmth, and hunkered deeper into his duster.

The cold dark fit Jim Taylor's mood. He'd left camp at four a.m., fueled only by reheated coffee and granola bars. Bob had sent him off on this errand because the campers, Chet Stevens, Jr., to be exact, had insisted on special supplies for his wife's birthday dinner. This meant a four hour ride down to the trailhead, a hundred mile round trip drive to the nearest big town, and a four hour ride back up. All in one day and back to camp in time for "cocktails." Silly ass, spoiled rich people.

Bob's camp was in the middle of the Big Horn wilderness. The campers were surrounded by majestic mountains, awesome trout streams, and miles and miles of untouched forest. Two days in camp and all they did was piss and moan about no television, no hot running water, and spotty cell phone service. Why come to the wilderness if all you're going to do is complain about it? These people were idiots, rich twits who served no useful function in society except, he supposed, to spend gobs of money. He suspected that Bob agreed to send him on this errand so Jim wouldn't tell Stevens to screw himself.

He'd practically begged Bob to take him on as an assistant for the pack trips, told him he'd work for free. When Bob had asked him why he'd left his home and business, Jim had mumbled something about just needing a break, that it was no big deal. Jim knew he hadn't fooled Bob, but Bob was a good enough friend to not press him. He should have known that helping Bob entailed more than taking care of horses and doing camp chores. He just wasn't up to dealing with people, especially assholes.

He sighed. At least he'd have this day to himself. Solitude. That was why he'd come to these mountains. Pleased to be where he was and not where he'd come from.

Chapter 2

Archer Mesa trailhead was deserted when Jim forded the creek and rode in. The sky was a clear royal blue and the morning sun had burned off the early chill. He scanned the area.

The trailhead was in a grassy bowl formed by Archer Mesa to the south, a steep rocky ridge to the north, and a half mile slope back up to the plateau he'd just descended. Peeking beyond the slope were the snow speckled mountains, clear and shining in the slanting sunlight. The grass on the meadows and slopes was dry, browned by sun and lack of rain.

He rode up to the wood fenced corral, dismounted, and unsaddled the horse and mule. He put them in the corral and found hay in Bob's trailer. After he threw them a bale he gave Buck a good grooming.

"Okay, Buck, you get some down time while I run into town. I'll be back in a couple hours."

The horse raised his head and looked Jim in the eye. After a moment Buck nodded, let out a grunt, and went back to eating.

He walked over to the little shack used by the trailhead

host hoping to cadge a cup of coffee. He was out of luck. A note on the door informed him that the host was in town until noon.

Jim walked back to the trailer and unhitched it from the truck. He was about to get in and drive off when a squad car came cruising up the gravel access road. The car rolled into the trailhead and came to a stop next to the trailer. As the dust settled a mountain of a man got out.

The mountain strode up to Jim, towering over his six foot, rail thin frame.

"Howdy. I'm Zeke Thomasen, Sheriff of Flint County. Are you the fella who works for Bob Lundsten?"

Battered boots stuck out from his jeans and his tan, snap button shirt sported the metal badge of his office. Six foot five and over two hundred sixty pounds with a rugged, weather beaten face, he looked like the kind of western lawman who would break up barroom fights single handed and stare down gunslingers. Jim immediately thought "John Wayne." The sheriff had some hard miles on him, probably about sixty five years' worth by Jim's reckoning, but his eyes were bright and alert under his white Stetson. Jim liked him on sight.

Jim stepped forward and shook hands.

"Yes, sir. I'm Jim Taylor. Refugee from Wisconsin. Down here on a fool's errand for some campers who have more money than sense."

The sheriff snorted. "I've told Bob I can't see how he can put up with taking care of folks like that."

"Sheriff, I'm coming to that point myself. What brings you out here?"

"You heard about the big protest over at Flat Top Mountain? Lot of folks don't want oil drilling there.

We've got eco people, green people, and a lot of local elk hunters trying to stop it. That area is a prime elk breeding ground."

"Yes, sir. I've heard a bit about it from Bob. Personally, I'm sympathetic." Jim smiled and shrugged. "But, um, I'm new here and figure I should keep my head down and stay out of trouble."

"Good, keep it that way." The sheriff raised an eyebrow. "I see you've got a gun on your hip."

"Yes, sir. Bob's rule. I've got it in case I need to put an animal down. Can't just call the vet like back home."

"You sure do use 'sir' a lot. You ex-military?"

Jim laughed. "No, just habit I guess. I was a lawyer back home, almost called you 'Your Honor'. Once you get chewed out by some cranky old judge, you learn to do it without thinking."

The sheriff shook his head. "Huh, a lawyer? What are you doing babysitting spoiled tourists? Running from something?" The sheriff gave Jim a penetrating look.

"Sheriff, it's a long story," he put his hands up, palms out, "but nothing criminal." And nothing I want to talk about.

"Well, anyway, I'm here to warn you and Bob. We've got the access road to Flat Top blocked off, don't want the protesters mixing with the drilling crew."

"What's that got to do with us?"

"I'm afraid some of them might come up your way and get at Flat Top from behind. I need you to let me know if you see folks trying to do that."

"You can get there from the Solitude trail?"

"Yep. Go over Florence Pass and then head west five miles then south. Take a couple of days on foot."

"Okay, Sheriff, I'll let Bob know as soon as I get what I was sent for."

"What was that?"

"Champagne, brie cheese, goose liver pate, and genuine table water crackers."

The sheriff laughed and shook his head. "Jim, you give Bob my sympathy."

Chet Stevens, Jr., had climbed part way up the ridge behind the camp. He had his cell phone to his ear.

"Okay. It's in motion. I'll call when…" He stopped when he saw movement below him.

"Chet, what are you doing up here?" His wife, Stella, stepped into view fifteen yards away. "Who are you calling?"

"Call you later," Chet whispered and shut the phone quickly. He stuffed it into a pants pocket. "Hi, Hon."

"Chet, who were you calling?" she asked impatiently.

"Just trying to make a business call, but even climbing way up here the cell service sucks." He tried to put a frustrated look on his face, grimacing and slumping his shoulders in an exaggerated fashion.

"You have people to manage things," she snapped. "The boys are making too much noise. I think I'm getting a migraine." She rubbed her temples for emphasis. "Why don't you take them fishing?"

Chet stuck both hands in his pockets to hide his clenched fists. "Okay, I'll get the guide to take us."

Chapter 3

As he was watering the horse and mule at the creek, Jim stretched and tried to get the kinks out of his sixty year old body. Eight hours in the saddle. He was due back in camp but, screw it, he thought, he needed a break. He sighed and took a swig from his canteen.

The Big Horns were Jim's Eden. He was enthralled by the mountains, loved the beauty and peace he always found there. The beauty of the wilderness and the companionship of his horse were all he needed and desired. He needed to be free of all the crap he had accumulated in his life, free to be himself, not what others expected of him.

He took in his surroundings while the sun warmed his back. They were about twenty yards off the Solitude Trail and ten yards below in a tangle of moose brush. The creek sparkled in the sunlight as it rushed unstoppably in the iron grip of gravity, taking melt water down to the arid plains miles below. Thickly wooded ridges hemmed him in and up slope sheer cliffs and granite, snow streaked peaks loomed, watching in their majestic indifference. He and the animals were puny, like ants, in this huge, wild organism, their needs and worries and lives meant nothing here.

He listened to the rush and gurgle of the creek and the slurping of the animals drinking. A breeze made the aspen leaves rattle and wafted the scent of pine pollen. A ditty ran through his head making him chuckle. "Summer breeze makes me feel fine, blowing through the jasmine in my mind."

Suddenly the animals stiffened and looked up from the rushing water. What? He looked around, saw nothing that would alert them. Then Jim heard it too, the high pitched whine of small engines. The sound augered through his head like a dentist's drill, shattering his reverie. "What the fuck?"

He had never before heard the sound of engines in this wilderness zone. All engines, even chainsaws, were prohibited by the Forest Service. He shook his head and grimaced. Jim looked at his horse who had turned his head toward the noise, ears pricked, eyes alert.

"Shit."

The horse blew a raspberry, spraying water on Jim.

"Nice, thanks for the shower."

Engines in the wilderness were more than an intrusion. Pollution was more accurate. To Jim it was like somebody taking a crap on his front steps.

He wondered if this intrusion could be the protesters the sheriff warned about, but no, driving machines into the wilderness didn't fit with environmental consciousness. What then?

Jim peeked out when the machines went past. He thought about confronting them. Six of them, ATVs, one guy on each with a load of gear strapped behind, rifles slung across their shoulders. "Oops." Not a wise move. Reminded him of drunk flatlanders from Chicago invading the north woods of Wisconsin during deer season, tossing bottles and cans

8

where ever they went, shooting at road signs, trespassing, and generally acting like assholes who thought nothing of fouling a pristine place. The world was their trashcan.

He grimaced. "Christ, armed jackasses. What's going on?"

Jim, Buck, and the pack mule were almost back to Bob Lundsten's wilderness camp. The pack mule was loaded with the supplies he had been sent to get. Camp was about a mile up the trail, across Clear Creek, and tucked away on a pine covered hill. Bob was at camp with the Stevens party.

He felt a tingling between his shoulder blades. Jim sensed some primitive part of his brain go on full alert. Six guys with rifles driving through the wilderness. Hunting season was months away and those machines would scare game off anyway. Fucking flatlanders. They were somebody's bad news. Maybe they were tied into the protest. Guns at a protest could end in disaster. He needed to alert the sheriff and he should warn Bob. But camp was up the trail in the same direction that the machines were headed.

He mounted up. "Buck, time to get moving."

The horse turned his head, looked Jim in the eye, and snorted.

"Yeah, we've got to, you get to rest and eat at camp."

He decided to keep his distance. He'd head for camp but not on the trail. He hoped the men would just pass on by the camp. He would call the sheriff and then he could forget about them just like he was trying to forget about everything that had driven him here. He was here to live a new, simple life. The last thing he needed was a bunch of armed yahoos buzzing around and fouling this paradise.

They went up and over the trail, leading the pack mule. Jim let the horse pick his way up a slight slope to the top of a small wooded ridge, twenty yards on the other side of the trail. Buck found a game trail that paralleled the trail the ATV's had taken. They could easily hear the engines ahead.

It was gloomy under the pines. The game trail meandered around the trees. Jim had to look back to make sure the mule followed the same line as the horse so she wouldn't take the wrong way around a tree and snag the lead rope and yank it out of his hand. Mules could be perverse and he didn't need the aggravation right now.

About half way to camp the gloom got gloomier. The sun disappeared, the sky blackened. Buck twitched his ears. Jim shivered in a sudden drop in temperature. First a hiss, then rain drops through the gaps in the trees, then a steady rain. Storms came quickly in the mountains. Jim halted the horse, turned, and got his duster from behind the saddle. He shrugged his way into it and hunched down under his hat.

When they got even with the camp, Jim stopped Buck. They could no longer hear the engine noise. Just as they started to relax, they heard shouting up ahead. About a hundred yards through the pine woods was Deer Lake.

"Oh shit, Buck. I bet Bob took the campers for some fishing at the lake. We better take a peek."

He tied the mule to a big tree and he and Buck followed the game trail towards the lake. When they got near the edge of the trees, they halted. Jim nudged Buck a couple of paces to where they had a clear view of the lake but stayed within the tree line. He mentally shrugged at his caution.

The lake stretched before them for about a hundred yards. The near shore was deserted, but there were figures at the far end of the lake where the trail passed its outlet to the creek. Jim got his binoculars out of the saddle bag.

He picked out Bob and several of the campers. The ATVs had stopped there. The rain was coming down hard. One of the campers, Chet Stevens, was waving his arms at the men on the ATVs, making shooing gestures. Bob was about ten yards back holding onto the two children. Eve, the nanny, hovered behind. Dave, the Stevens' assistant was moving to get between Chet and the men.

Buck gave a low grumble.

"Yeah, Buck, this is trouble. That idiot Stevens. He's going to piss off this bunch. What a dumbass." One of those rich guys who thought their wealth gave them immunity from harm.

Chet Stevens must have really lipped off. One of the men shoved him and Stevens stumbled backwards, arms windmilling, and landed flat on his back. Jim saw Dave gather himself. He'd wondered about Dave. Chet and Stella Stevens called him their assistant, but he didn't seem to do any assisting. Muscular, crew cut, always wearing mirrored shades, Dave just seemed to watch. Hadn't said five words the whole time they'd been in camp.

Dave jumped forward and grabbed the guy, twisted, and threw him to the ground.

Jim muttered, "No, no, no."

Another of the men took his rifle off his shoulder and clubbed Dave on the back of his head with the stock. Dave lurched forward and collapsed in a heap.

Everyone seemed to pause for a few seconds. Jim could hear nothing except the hiss of the rain. He relaxed a little, hoping that this would be the end of it and the strangers would get on their machines and leave. Chet and Dave could lick their wounds. Chet would rant and rave over dinner. Jim would struggle to hold his tongue.

Then the man, big, burly, and bald, walked over to Dave and kicked him in the side. Dave crawled a few feet and then got up on his hands and knees trying to get up. "Just stay down. They've got guns. Don't be stupid."

The big, bald guy slowly raised his rifle and fired at him point blank. Dave collapsed. The kids screamed. Then the man fired again.

Man and horse flinched. The shots echoed off the cliffs on either side of the valley.

"Holy shit," Jim shuddered. "This can't be happening." As much to reassure himself as the horse, he stroked Buck's neck and whispered "You're okay, you're okay. They don't know about us."

The big guy turned and pointed the rifle at Bob. Bob raised his hands, palms out. The guy gestured toward Chet who was curled on the ground. Two of the others picked him up and set him on his feet.

Jim and Buck watched as the killers herded Bob, Stevens, and the kids toward the camp at gunpoint, leaving Dave's body where it lay.

Buck looked back at Jim. Jim slowly shook his head. He swallowed and took a deep breath.

"Okay, Buck, let's see what they do."

Jim had Buck jog trot back to the ridge. From the cover of the trees, they watched the campers wade across the creek, Bob and Eve carrying the kids. The killers drove their machines across. Then they all went up the hill to Bob's camp.

The rain came down harder.

Chapter 4

He sat there on the horse in the rain, stunned.

He stared into the distance, not seeing. He'd had a premonition of trouble but hadn't expected anything like this. He clenched his hands into fists to stop them shaking and tried to slow his breathing.

He swallowed, his mouth dry. He had to do something. He was the only person who could do anything about what had just happened. "Jesus." It was up to him. He couldn't run away from this like he'd run away from everything else. Bob and the campers could be killed next. He must not let them down.

Jim closed his eyes and fought his fear. He knew he was close to panic. "If I panic I'm useless. Those people need me. Come on, Jim, get a grip. Or you will fail. Think! Think this through."

A man was dead. This wasn't a television show or a movie. It had really happened. Now his friend Bob and the campers were hostages. "Oh, fuck me. What am I going to do?" He leaned forward in the saddle and patted the horse's neck.

He had to do something, but he was frozen, his mind

trying to catch up with what they'd just seen. All he could think of were questions. What was going on? Why did this happen? Who are those guys? What am I supposed to do? They were miles from the trailhead and any help. They were getting soaked. There were six armed men just across the creek. "Slow down, Jim. Look at your options."

He couldn't ride back to the trailhead, it would take four hours. It would be the dead of night when he got to it and no one would be there. The trailhead, the sheriff. He would call the sheriff. He got his cell phone from a saddle bag.

No bars, no service. Shit. He'd have to climb the ridge.

Before he could hike the ridge he had to see to the horse and mule. What about them? Couldn't let them wander while he went off.

He looked at Buck. He was a smart, experienced horse. Jim could count on him, needed him. What about the mule? With Buck he could be quick and stealthy, the mule, however, was an impediment. Movement would be clumsy bringing the mule along. A loaded pack mule was noisy in the woods, unloaded the mule would be surplus.

Buck looked over at Jim, gave a low grumble, and tossed his head toward the mule.

"Buck, you read my mind. We'll turn the mule loose. She'll make her way back to the trailhead corral."

Jim knew that Bob's mules had been on this trail many times and knew their way. Once they were pointed back towards the trailhead, the mules were eager to get to the corral. The corral meant food and no work. He was confident that this mule would find her way. He unloaded the mule, piling the panniers under a large pine. He left the pack saddle on the mule. Jim found paper and pen in his saddle bag and quickly

14

wrote "Tell sheriff murder near Lundsten camp. Hostages taken. Will try to call on cell phone. Jim Taylor." He wrapped this in a plastic baggie and tied it to one of the saddle yokes. He knew that during the day there was a volunteer worker at the trail head. This guy would see the mule in the morning and know something was wrong. If he couldn't get through on the phone this would be better than nothing.

Jim untied the mule and slapped her on the rump. "Follow your nose Annie. Go home." The mule wandered off in the right direction.

He took stock of what he had. He wore his duster, hat, and chaps. In his saddle bags he had four granola bars, binoculars, matches, lighter, a topographical map, the cell phone, a spare shirt, an insulated vest, and spare ammo for his 38 which he had in a holster on his hip. A fine kit for a day ride in the mountains, but lacking much for an overnight camp in the rain.

Most importantly, he had Buck. Buck was a ten year old bay quarter horse gelding, fifteen hands high. His coat was a deep, glossy mahogany and his long, thick mane and tail were jet black. He had been a reining show horse for six years when Jim bought him. They had instantly hit it off and had become fast friends. Buck was smart, quick, and extremely well trained.

He led Buck to the shelter of a clump of tall pines and tied him on a long lead. Then he dragged the mule's panniers over and the tarp which had covered them. Inside was a fifty pound bag of horse feed cubes, a canteen full of water, a cooler which held the champagne, cheese, pate, and crackers, and a 12-pack of Bud, which he'd bought for his own cocktail hour, and a big can of Spaghettios for the little boys.

15

The rain was not quitting and it was getting cold. Jim tied the tarp to some low branches near the horse and gathered everything under the shelter. He sat for a minute to gather his wits. It was time to climb and try to reach the sheriff. Keeping busy had distracted him from what he had seen. Best to keep doing something, he wasn't ready to really think about this disaster.

He made a pile of the horse cubes within reach of the horse. Then he scrambled back up to the top of the ridge to check on the camp. Visibility was not good, but he could smell the smoke from Bob's cook tent. He heard nothing but the hiss of the rain. He reckoned nobody would be going anywhere in this downpour. Those bastards now had a warm and dry place to wait out the weather.

Chapter 5

The slope was steep and slippery in the rain. The trees were thick, clumped together, and mixed with tangles of brush. His duster kept getting hung up on snags. It took over a half hour to get high enough to get good service. He was sweating and cursing when he halted.

He called 911 and said he needed the Flint County Sheriff's office. They put him through to dispatch.

"I've just seen a murder and kidnapping. There are hostages. Armed men. Got to talk to the sheriff. It's Jim Taylor."

"Calm down, sir. The sheriff's in the building."

Put him on hold! Jesus H. Christ! He wanted to scream. "Come on, come on. Unbelievable, murder and kidnapping and they put me on hold," he growled. He started pacing in a circle, stopped, and kicked at the ground. He grabbed a pine bough, plucked the needles off one by one. Minutes were ticking by. He tried to calm himself, slow his breathing.

Finally, "Jim, this is Zeke Thomasen. What's going on?"

"Sheriff, I thought they might be protesters like you said," he blurted. "They shot Dave and took everybody. We need help up here."

"Slow down. Nice and easy. From the beginning." The sheriff was cool and calm.

Jim took a deep breath and blew it out.

"Okay. I was just coming back to camp when these six guys came by on ATVs. Rifles on their backs. They met Bob and the campers by Deer Lake. They shot Dave. He was the Stevens' assistant. He was on the ground when they shot him. Then they took Bob and the family back to camp. They're holed up there now. That's all I know." He sighed. It was a relief to get it all out.

"There's one dead and the others are hostages?"

"Yeah, I saw it. Jesus. Shot him twice. In front of the kids."

"Where are you?"

"I'm on the other side of the creek. They're all at the camp. I can't tell what's going on over there."

"I got you. Any more gunshots?"

"Nope. I'd have heard. Nothing. You've got to do something. They've got Bob and the family. When can you get here?"

"Jim, I can't get my men up there until tomorrow. They're all over by Flat Top and it's going to be dark soon."

Jim's heart sank. He groaned. The sheriff was talking again.

"Can you describe these men?"

"I only watched the one guy, the one who did the shooting. He was big, almost your height, heavy build, bald head. Bastard. Sorry, that's the best I can do. Can't you get up here tonight?" He was pleading. Stop it. The sheriff was right, it would be dark soon. He couldn't ride up here blind, especially with that bunch nearby.

"No can do. Jim, I need you to hang in there, be my eyes

18

and ears. Can you stay hidden and keep an eye on them? Let me know if anything happens? You'll have to be there all night and report to me first thing tomorrow."

Jim took a deep breath, blew it out. It was up to him, nobody else. He shut his eyes and bowed his head.

"Jim, you still there?"

"Yes, sir, I can and I will. Give me your direct line and I'll call in the morning. Don't bother trying to call me, I have to climb a ridge to get through."

"Good man. I'm going to see what might be going on from this end. What's the name of the campers again?"

"Chet Stevens, Jr., wife is Stella. Two young boys and a nanny named Eve."

"Got it. Okay, Jim. I'll talk with you in the morning. Be careful."

"Yes, sir." Be careful. Yeah, thanks a lot.

Chapter 6

Jim staggered and slid back down the ridge. He was totally on his own. Time to 'cowboy up' as Bob would say.

He tried not to think about what was happening in the camp. Seven, no six innocent people at the mercy of six armed killers. Nothing he could do for them right now. Best thing to do was to take care of his horse.

He went back to Buck and unsaddled him. Then he led him back a ways, crossed the trail, and went down to the creek so they both could drink. "Drink up, Buck. We'll get you more cubes when we're done here." He drank straight from the creek, kneeling next to the horse.

He squatted next to the creek, oblivious to the rain. Rail thin, his brown hair and beard were streaked with gray. He'd been a trial lawyer back in Wisconsin, out here in the Big Horns to start a new life, escape the mess he'd made of his former life. He loved this wilderness, the peace and solitude never failed to refresh and center him. Nothing in his life had prepared him for this disaster. Now the solitude frightened him. He was totally on his own. He groaned. He needed to sort things out and calm down. He needed a sounding board.

Buck interrupted his slurping with a loud snort.

Jim looked over at his horse. The horse looked back at him then resumed his drinking.

He had Buck.

He wasn't alone.

"What are these guys doing up here? Are they bank robbers running from the law? White supremacist nut jobs looking to set up their own little fortress up here? Whatever it is, it was well planned; they're all armed, have lots of gear, and ride ATV's."

The horse raised his head and turned to Jim, water dribbling from his chin.

"Buck, we've just seen them kill someone in cold blood, so Bob and the campers could well be next and we can't stop them." Jim knew he was babbling, couldn't stop himself. "The sheriff wants us to wait here and keep watch for him. Maybe there'll be a chance to help. Those guys were heading up the trail. There's nothing and no one up that way. The trail goes up to Florence Pass but there's nothing up there for a bunch of killers, only more trails."

"We've got to hope that they will keep going up for whatever reason. So we wait them out. Stay hidden and wait."

Jim looked over at Buck. Buck looked right back, then snorted.

"What's on your mind? You know I'm repeating myself because I'm scared? Well, I am. It's just you and me up here and a band of killers for neighbors."

Buck snorted again.

"Some folks might think I've gone off my rocker, Buck, but I think I'd explode or something if I didn't talk this through. Better to talk with you than talk to myself." He paused. Talking had calmed him. It was time to settle down for the night.

As always on the east side of the Big Horns, it got dark quickly. It also got cold. After stuffing himself with brie, pate, and beer, Jim made himself a bed. He used the empty canvas panniers as a ground cloth. He put on his extra shirt and the vest then snapped closed every snap on his duster and covered himself with the tarp.

He was damp, cold, and scared. He couldn't get comfortable, couldn't get warm. He hugged himself and curled into a fetal position to conserve body heat. He listened to the rain – it was letting up. Buck was grunting and munching a few feet away. The woods around them was still, the only noise close by was the dripping of the moisture from the trees and bushes, the creek shushing and gurgling in the background. Under other circumstances, Jim would have found these noises soothing, but the cold and his self doubt made it impossible to relax.

"Buck, I'm an idiot. I have no business spying on a bunch of bastards. We're stuck here for the night. Let's hope the sheriff gets here early."

Buck looked over at Jim. Jim had never met a horse that had such an intelligent look in his eye. Buck nickered. He seemed to say, "I am with you no matter what you decide to do."

Jim was not afraid of the wilderness. He had camped up here many times over the years and ridden most of the trails in this part of the Big Horns. He was not a violent man, had never struck anyone in anger. He wasn't even a hunter. As he'd told the sheriff, the 38 he had was for putting a horse down in an emergency. Something he hoped he never had to do, but in the wilderness one couldn't call the vet to come and euthanize a horse with a broken leg.

Having Buck with him gave Jim courage. Whatever was ahead he would not have to face alone. He had no idea what he would need to do tomorrow, but he knew he couldn't run away from this mess. He had to do what he could for his friend and for the camper family.

He'd told everyone that he was going to Wyoming to help his friend Bob and catch some rest and relaxation, a kind of get away from it all sabbatical. In truth he had been close to eating a bullet and he'd come here to try living like Peter Pan, to not be a grown up any more and maybe stay in this Never Never Land. He hoped to find his real self, a thing buried in the distractions of his former life.

The mountains let him push all the crap into the back rooms of his mind. Existence here was immediate, living in the moment. Responsibilities were basic, do camp chores and take care of your horse.

Now none of that mattered.

Jim yawned and shivered. He was so tired. He was so cold. He could feel both in his bones. He had to sleep. He reached over and grabbed the saddle pad and folded it for a pillow, covered his head with the tarp and tried not to think about the cold. He inhaled deeply, got a good, strong whiff of horse sweat from the saddle pad. It relaxed him.

Sitting on a hay bale dressed in tattered jeans and a Greatful Dead t-shirt, he'd been cleaning a hand gun. A warm breeze brought the scent of lilacs as butterflies and hummingbirds danced over the flowers alongside the barn. Jim was oblivious to this beauty, his full attention on the gun. He looked down each cylinder of the revolver, shiny little tunnels, clean and smooth with a faint whiff of Hoppe's solvent.

Everything had been piling up. It was like a leaky boat. He'd plug one hole and there'd be two more in its place. His ship was sinking. He'd devoted almost forty years to his law practice and had achieved success in the courtroom and respect of his peers. But he was at the brink of ruin.

The day before he'd been served with a delinquency notice and lien by the IRS. It was like a punch in the gut. He had no way to pay it. He was always juggling debts, wondering how he was going to pay next week's bills. There was no end in sight. It would go on like this until he died of old age, retirement was a pipe dream. He was on a treadmill. His finances were fucking hopeless. He was so fucking tired of always worrying about money, paying bills.

If the IRS didn't take his farm, his soon to be ex-wife, his third, surely would. Janelle had called him that morning. He'd asked her if she was coming back. She exploded, gave vent to her pent up rage. Literally screamed at him. He was an aloof, insensitive bastard. She wanted him out of her life and she was going to take him for everything. She kept going but he tuned her out, just shut down. She finished the call with a "fuck you, Jim," and hung up.

When he got to the office there was a letter from his doctor with the results of the endoscopy: he had a bleeding ulcer. His body was betraying him. He took pills for arthritis, herbs for his prostate, and any day now he'd be taking Geritol. At sixty one it would only get worse. Next it would be assisted living, then a nursing home, drooling, adult diapers. Shit, The Who had it right.

Worst of all was the call about Julia Schultz. She'd taken an overdose and died in her sleep. She had called him the day before and he'd avoided her, had the receptionist shunt her to voice mail. He'd let her down. He knew she was fragile, he just didn't want to be bothered. Ah, man. Now she was dead. There was no do over. Her death was on him. Pride in his work, caring for his clients, had always been the rock of his self respect. Now even that was gone, replaced by shame and guilt.

The gun. It would be so easy. All that shit would be gone, the guilt, the failures, the responsibilities. There would be peace.

He hefted the gun. Such a simple thing. It had the power to solve everything. He spun the empty cylinders. Just load it, stick it in his mouth, pull the trigger.

He was so fucking tired of being responsible. Being responsible just brought failures, debts, old age. He'd wasted his life being responsible. His life was being ground up into dust. That's what being responsible got him.

Country Joe ran through his head. "Who am I to sit and wait while the wheels of fate slowly grind my life away?"

He sat there and closed his eyes. It seemed like it was the right thing to do. If it wasn't, it wouldn't matter.

And then he heard Buck whinny out in the pasture.

Chapter 7

It was hot in the tent. The air was close and stank of bacon grease, unwashed bodies, and wet clothes, like a locker room inside a kitchen. A collapsible wood burning stove blazed near the entrance flaps. Three Coleman lanterns hung from a pole that ran along the ceiling.

The captives were sitting sprawled on the floor. The adults were bound hand and foot. The two boys, Ricky, age seven, and Randy, almost five, had their hands tied. Both were half asleep in the stifling heat, their faces streaked with tears. Stella and Eve had the boys between them and cuddled them as best they could.

Chet Stevens, Jr., slouched against the tent wall, his face blank and eyes unfocused. His lips were moving but no sound escaped. Bob Lundsten had his head bent toward his chest, eyes apparently closed. He seemed asleep, but he was not.

Four of their captors sat at a folding table drinking beer and playing cards. They talked quietly and looked over at the captives from time to time. All were young, early twenties, and sported various facial piercings. They were bulked up, heavily muscled, but moved stiffly, without grace. Their faces were puffy and pimpled, looked like steroid abusers. Bob watched them through slitted eyelids.

He was trying to sort out what had happened and why. It did not seem like a random meeting at the lake, almost like these men were looking for the Stevens family. He knew Chet Stevens was wealthy, connected with the oil and gas industry somehow. Was this a kidnapping? The whole family? Maybe. Whatever was going on, Bob knew he would have to make himself useful or he'd be dead.

He was responsible for the safety of his campers. That was always his first priority on a pack trip. But this was beyond his control. He could think of nothing he'd done to bring this about and nothing he could do to protect the campers.

And then there was Jim. He was long overdue. None of the men had mentioned meeting anyone on the trail, but that meant nothing. Jim could be dead just like Dave. If they hadn't met Jim then there was hope. If Jim learned of the situation he would get help. Yet help might not be a good thing. He and the campers would be hostages if the sheriff came.

One of the little boys, Randy, started whining. "I want the Spaghettios," he sniveled. "I want them now. Jim promised to bring them."

Eve tried to hush him but it was too late, the damage had been done.

One of the men at the table leaned over and asked "Who's this Jim? Where is he?"

The other boy spoke up. "Mr. Bob's helper. He went to town today."

The man stood up quickly and left the tent.

Bob groaned silently. Jim was alive and probably getting help, but now their captors knew.

Chapter 8

Two men stood under a huge pine, its thick branches sheltering them from the rain. The shadows made them almost invisible to anyone approaching, but they had a clear view of the cook tent, the lanterns making it a beacon in the rainy gloom.

Big Jack Bulganin had been talking with Botts, his right hand man. Both were ex-military and former mercenaries. Big Jack was big. Six foot four and close to two hundred seventy pounds of solid muscle, he was in his late thirties. Almost totally bald, he shaved off the bits of remaining hair for appearance's sake. Botts was his opposite. Short and wiry, he had his black hair in a pony tail. Both had a watchfulness, an acute alertness in their eyes, a stare like a bird of prey.

When Big Jack heard what the little boys said he sent the man back with orders to bring Chet Stevens to him. When the man had left, he turned to Botts.

"Fuck. If that guy catches on to what's happened, he'll run for help. We'll get surrounded. We've got to change the plan. The cops will know where we are. We'll have to move and rework the schedule."

Two men dragged Chet over to Big Jack and Botts. Still bound hand and foot, the men held him up by the armpits.

"Leave him and go back inside. Question the others," Jack ordered.

They dropped Chet who crumpled to the ground.

After the men left, Big Jack squatted next to Chet and untied him.

"Is it true, there's a helper?"

"Yeah, due back from town before now. Fetching supplies I ordered."

"Shit. Why didn't you tell me sooner?"

"No chance. The others were always around. They can't know I'm in on this."

Chapter 9

Hoping to catch a late arriving helper, Big Jack had Botts detail two men to stand guard outside. Told them to shoot anyone they saw. The men grumbled about the cold and the rain but shut up when Jack growled at them.

"You want to be mercs? It's not always warm and sunny. Suck it up."

The two young men stood at the top of the hill huddled under their ponchos. It was gloomy, the rain steady, and the temperature was dropping. They were totally exposed on the hill top.

"Hey, Fritz," whispering, "Big Jack is one mean mother fucker." He looked back toward camp. "You saw how he blew that poor sucker away."

Fritz leaned close to his friend. "Yeah, man. Freaked me out. The guy was down and unarmed, totally helpless." He looked over his shoulder. "No way I'm gonna cross Big Jack."

The two men huddled there for a couple of minutes,

miserable in the cold rain. Each lost in thought, useless as sentries.

Fritz cleared his throat, spat. "Look, Larry, we hired on as help on a mission. Learn about being contractors. They didn't say anything about killing anybody. I didn't sign up for that."

"Yeah, but what're we gonna do?" Larry swallowed. "You think Big Jack will kill the others?"

Fritz grabbed his shoulder. "Larry, I think we're in deep shit. We're fucked."

Larry hung his head. "Fuck."

Big Jack and Botts took Chet fifty yards into the trees. They were invisible to anyone without night goggles. The three sat on a fallen tree trunk and thrashed things out.

Chet was an unimposing figure. He was soft with a pouty mouth, weak chin, and a tidy little mustache. Only in his early forties, he had a gut that hung over his belt. A flashy pinky ring, a gold Rolex, and professionally styled hair gave him the look of a rich fop.

"Your guy didn't have to shove me so hard. I think I blew a disc."

"Tough shit. It had to look convincing. Our problem is that helper." Jack chewed on a knuckle, narrowed his eyes. "The plan was to hold everybody here and ransom the whole family. Keep it secret, no cops. Can't do that now. We're going to have to move."

"Yeah, Jack, I know. But you can't move the whole family. You've got to leave Stella and the kids here. And you killed Dave. Now it's murder, not just kidnapping. We were going to keep this under the radar. How can we do that now?" Chet was wringing his hands and starting to whine.

"Shut up. You hired me for this job. I run it the way I see fit. That Dave was a problem. He had to go sooner or later. He'd have figured it out."

Chet stared off into the gloom. He blew out a breath and shook his head.

Jack and Botts exchanged a look.

Jack stood, towering over Chet. "It's done. Time to move on."

Chet hung his head, "Okay, so now what?"

"We make the ransom call tonight and we move in the morning. We take you and head for where the van is parked."

"We still going to have the ransom brought to the mountains?"

"Yeah, if we set up at the spot in advance nobody can watch the drop or try to follow us."

"I'm getting fucking wet and cold out here. Let's get the call done and get me back in the tent."

Jack looked over at Botts.

"Go get the satellite phone. We'll make the call before it's totally dark."

Botts slipped off noiselessly into the shadows, his movements smooth, catlike.

When Botts came back Jack handed the phone to Chet.

"Okay, you know where to call and what to say? Remember, don't answer questions, just say what happened and give the phone to me."

Chet keyed in his father's private number. His father answered on the third ring.

"Stevens. Who's on my private line?"

32

"Dad, it's me. I'm in big trouble, so is the family, the boys." His quiver was not entirely faked. His father still intimidated him at age forty.

"What? Chet, what's going on?"

Big Jack took the phone.

"Stevens, this is Friends of the Elk. Listen very carefully. I won't repeat this. We have your son and his wife and kids. Right now they're safe. It's up to you to keep it that way. Understand?"

"Who are you? What is this?" The elder Stevens' voice was stern, angry.

"Shut up. This is the Friends of the Elk. We have Chet, Junior, and his family. Do you want them killed?"

"No. Put Chet on."

"Maybe later. Here's what you'll do. Pull your men and equipment from Flat Top Mountain. Cancel your lease with the Forest Service. I want written confirmation from the District Ranger. Then you're going to deliver that and ten million dollars where and when I tell you. No cops. I even smell a cop and I start killing your family. Stay by this phone. I will call with instructions. Is that clear?"

"Yes. Let me speak with my son."

Jack held the phone near Chet and nodded.

"Dad," breathless, "they've got me and Stella and the boys. You've got to do what they say. They've killed Dave, they're going to kill us."

Jack shut the phone down.

Chapter 10

The horse liked the mountains. Basically a curious soul, he savored this change of scene. Before Jim he had been on the show circuit, either trailering to a show, performing, or training, a very structured life. When he came to live with Jim life slowed down. Jim rode him frequently but otherwise he was allowed to graze in a large pasture and visit with the mares across the fence. A part of him missed the excitement of performing at shows, seeing new stables, watching other performers, but he enjoyed this slower pace at Jim's farm and being outside free to graze.

The mountains were a totally new environment. It was hard work going up and down trails, but he was seeing a different world, deep forest, huge boulders, rushing creeks. He had forded creeks, wading into the rushing water and feeling around for sure footing. At first he had balked, but when he saw other horses do it he did it too. He had gained confidence about these new things in the weeks he and Jim had been in the mountains. And the smells were all new: the resinous pines and firs, the pungent reek of the mules, the strange musky odors of moose and elk.

He was devoted to this man, Jim. The man was kind and

gentle, never struck him, frequently groomed him. He was never overworked and was well fed. The man talked to him, treated him like a partner. He felt that this man understood when he expressed an opinion or responded to something the man said. Already an intuitive animal, his vocabulary was growing. He recognized names and places (barn, stall, hay, trailer) and directions (let's go, easy now, wait, you ready?).

The horse knew nothing about murder or failure or courage. Buck understood that something was very wrong. They had not returned to camp. He had smelled blood when they were near the lake. The horse had been on high alert ever since the machines had intruded with their noise and exhaust smell. Buck was sensitive to Jim's moods. He sensed the fear and anxiety in his man. He kept close watch on the man, waiting and ready.

Now, with the trees giving him some shelter, he was steaming away the wet in his coat. He had finished the feed cubes. He was tired and had a full belly. When his man settled down, Buck hung his head. To a casual observer he appeared to be asleep, but, as a prey animal, a part of his brain remained alert for danger.

Chapter 11

He woke shivering. His bladder was so distended and painful he groaned. He threw the tarp off and sat up. The night was pitch dark. He could barely see Buck, a shadow just a couple feet away, standing stock still, head down. He knew where he was, what had happened. The kidnappers hadn't found him. He jerked himself upright, walked a few paces, and relieved himself. Beyond the sheltering trees he could make out nothing. Except white! The ground was white. Snow. Not just a dusting. It was really coming down.

It was frigid. Nothing else mattered. He had lived in Wisconsin, so he was no stranger to cold, cold much worse than this. When it was twenty below he'd often thought about how horrible it would be to be trapped outside in the cold without enough clothes. What would he do? Now he was living that abstraction. It was worse than he had imagined. He needed to shout, to scream, but even in this near panic he dared not. He wanted to shrink inside himself and find warmth beneath his skin. Almost worse than the cold was the certain knowledge that there was no warm house in which to take refuge.

His feet were numb. His fingers burned. Everything muscle in his body was contracted, aching, cold. Jim shivered and hugged himself. His whole body was shaking, teeth chattering. He had to do something and soon or he would be shaking so hard he wouldn't be able to do anything. He'd lose control of his body. Then he'd fail, probably die of exposure. Through clenched teeth he let loose a string of curses, part moan, part growl. He started jogging in place. Couldn't do that all night.

The noise woke Buck who lifted his head and looked over at him.

"Sorry, don't mind me I'm just freezing to death. Go back to sleep. I'm going to risk a small fire. Nobody's going to wander over here in the snow."

Buck gave a horse mutter-huh, huh, huh-and dropped his head back down.

Hands shaking, Jim made a fire ring of rocks and gathered up pine needles and twigs from under the trees, digging down to get dry ones. Couldn't get the lighter working, then couldn't get the tinder to catch, his fingers stiff, clumsy. Come on, come on, catch, damn it. Finally found some scraps of paper in a pocket. Got the paper lit. The needles and twigs caught and flared. Carefully added little bits. At last he had a little fire going at the edge of his shelter. He added larger pieces of wood and got a good blaze going. Held his hands to the fire, finally a little warmth.

He was screened from the camp by the rise along the trail. They couldn't see the fire without crossing the creek. He doubted they'd do that at night. They might not even know about him and for sure wouldn't think anybody would spend the night out here without a tent.

He got out the can of Spaghettios and opened the top with his knife. He stuck the can in the fire and drank a beer. Gave it ten minutes and pulled the can out by the top. Ate the pasta with a flat stick. Cold on top, warm in the middle, and burnt on the bottom. It was delicious. Washed it down with more beer. He piled up more wood so he could keep the fire going.

He sat hunched by the fire, adding wood frequently. The fire helped his spirits but the parts of his body not facing it were ice cold. Most of the heat was dissipating, lost. Jim piled more rocks on the outside of the fire ring to reflect heat toward him. That didn't make much difference. Then he had an inspiration. He took the tarp off his shoulders and tied two corners to the pines he was sitting under. It formed a rough semi-circle around the fire.

The shelter worked. It captured enough heat. He wasn't exactly toasty but he didn't have to constantly shift to warm different parts of his body. He was still cold but it was bearable. His joints ached, but nothing was numb. The fire gave reassurance as well as warmth. He would survive. He tried to think of a plan for the morning, but he was just too tired and cold to focus. Watching the snow coming down and listening to the hiss when flakes hit the hot rocks mesmerized him. Eventually his eyes closed and he dropped off into a doze.

He saw the man shoot Dave. Then the killer shot Bob and the children. He watched himself walk up to the killer and without a word shoot him again and again. The killer laughed at him and just stood there while Jim kept shooting him.

Chapter 12

"Calm yourself down, Zeke. You've got to think this through. There's two messes to handle. You can't shoot from the hip this time."

Zeke Thomasen flopped down at his desk and looked out the window without seeing. He was in his last term of office. He figured he was getting too old for the job. There were lots of new folks in Flint County, city people who wanted the good life without all the problems of the cities. When they discovered that crime existed out here, they wanted big city type law enforcement: community relations officers, neighborhood patrols, college graduate police science majors in every squad car. Zeke knew that this brand of policing would come to Flint County, he was just too set in his ways to embrace it. Better to retire, raise a few head of cattle, and get some fishing in before they carted him off to some damn nursing home.

He'd hoped to finish out his career without a major crisis. That damn protest about Flat Top had ruined that plan. Drilling at that elk breeding ground had divided the community. Drilling meant jobs and jobs meant spending at local businesses. Opposing the drilling were not only the

39

ecology movement, but also local hunters and guides and those businesses who catered to hunters. Feelings ran high and arguments had turned physical at some bars.

He stood and began pacing, muttering to himself.

Damn, it was too late in the day to start up toward Bob Lundsten's camp. The trailhead was an hour drive from town and he guessed it would take four plus hours on horseback to the camp. Stupid to get there in the middle of the night. He could blunder right into the camp. Damn.

All his deputies were up at Flat Top helping the Forest Service keep the protesters in check. So far they had been orderly, but he knew things could get ugly in a hurry. Hell, he could ride up to the camp by himself at first light. Also stupid. He had to be smart. A family was held hostage. He'd have to pull men from the protest to deal with this murder. Nuts. What was going on up there? Was there a motive? Was it random? He needed background. He couldn't go in blind, not with innocents at risk.

What about that Jim Taylor? It was hard to fake how upset he was on the phone. Zeke saw no reason why Jim would lie about what had happened. But could he do what Zeke had asked? Or would he turn tail and run away?

The sheriff hollered out his open door, "Doris, is that young clerk still here? Find her and send her in to me."

He needed help, more personnel. It was time to call in a favor. He picked up his phone and called his old friend Jesse Walther, Chief of the State Patrol.

Jesse was in his office in Cheyenne.

"Zeke, you old devil. What's the latest in Flint County? You still have all those protesters? Bet you haven't been fishing this summer."

"Ah, Jesse, I'm getting too old for this. I've got a new headache. There's been a killing in the mountains and a family taken by the killers. I need to pull deputies from the protest and send them up there. Can you lend me some men to cover the protest?"

"Zeke, let me see what I can do. I'll call you back."

As Zeke hung up there was a knock on his door jamb. He waved the young woman in.

Sally Carter was a local girl home from college for the summer. She was built like a string bean--five foot six and barely a hundred pounds, arms and legs like pencils, a cross country runner at the University of Colorado. Her red hair was cut short, just covering her ears. To Zeke's eyes she looked about fifteen years old. This impression was reinforced by her pink Minnie Mouse t-shirt. She was smart and sharp with computers according to Doris.

"Sheriff, sir, you asked for me?" Her voice was soft, barely audible.

"Sally, I need your help. We've got a situation up in the mountains and I need some background information. I hear you're pretty handy with computers."

"Yes, sir. What can I do?"

Zeke Thomasen knew nothing about computers, was intimidated by them, and refused to learn how to use them. But he knew the things could be useful.

"Find out all you can about a guy named Chet Stevens, Jr., wife's name's Stella. Supposed to be wealthy. Look for any reason why someone would want to do him harm."

"Sure, can do. When do you need this?"

"Yesterday. I know it's after six. Lives are at stake. Take all the overtime you need."

"Yes, sir. Anything else?" She was bright eyed, eager, voice clear, no longer the meek little girl who'd walked in.

"Stop this 'sir' business. I've had enough of it today." The sheriff paused, thought back to the trailhead that morning. "One more thing. Check a guy named Jim Taylor, says he's a lawyer from Wisconsin."

"Okay, Sheriff."

"Go."

The young woman practically bounced out of the office.

Zeke sighed, wondered what it would be like to be twenty two again. "Huh, for starters I wouldn't have to deal with this mess," he muttered.

Doris poked her head into his office. "Sheriff, I've made a fresh pot of coffee. You need to eat. Can I get you something from the diner?"

"No, thanks, Doris. I've got too much on my mind to eat." He'd inherited Doris Wilburn when he took office. Nobody was quite sure when she'd started as the secretary for the department. She was a widow with grown children and teenage grandchildren. She looked after Zeke and the deputies as if they were family.

"Well, at least have some cookies. I brought them in today, oatmeal and raisin. I'll put them on your desk."

"Thanks, Doris. I'm going to step outside for a minute. Let me know when Jesse Walther calls."

Chapter 13

Zeke stood in the parking lot looking to the west along the highway that climbed into the mountains. The fresh air was clearing his headache. He could see a mass of rain clouds over a section of the mountains, could see the sheets of rain like gray curtains, guessed it was over where Bob's camp was. That Jim was going to have a miserable night. As he watched, the east face of the Big Horns grew darker and darker, becoming a mass of deep gray, details fading, lost until morning. The sky above the mountains was a pale blue, just a weak glow in the west above the highest peaks. He hated being down below, ignorant of what was happening, dependent on others for news. Every bit of him wanted to ride up there, get in the thick of it.

He heard the door behind him swing hard enough to hit the side of the building. Heard Doris clear her throat, an 'ahem' reminiscent of a stereotypical librarian. She looked the part, lips pursed, gray hair pulled back in a bun, glasses hanging on a beaded chain. She looked worried.

"Sheriff, phone for you. The Attorney General."

"Coming, I'll take it at my desk."

Albert Basset, III, was not one of his favorite people. In

fact, Zeke disliked the man but happily rarely had contact with him. Politician, expert ass kisser. Why was he calling now? He had the protest pretty much under control. When Al Basset called it was never good news.

"Evening, Mr. Attorney General. What can Flint County do for you?"

"Sheriff, I've been notified of the situation up in the mountains."

Oh, crap. Jesse have you betrayed me? "What situation is that?"

"I've been called about the Stevens family's situation. The Governor and I are very concerned."

He hadn't used the name with Jesse. Someone else had called in the politicians. "Yes, sir. So am I. I'm waiting for backup from the state police so I can move my men from the Flat Top protest." He stared out the window at the darkened mountains, trying to picture the camp and the captive family.

"That's why I'm calling." Basset paused and Zeke stiffened, gripped the phone so hard that his knuckles turned white.

"You'll get no help from Chief Walther or any other state agency."

"What do you mean?" the Zeke was practically shouting into the phone.

"There's been a request to keep law enforcement away. I intend to honor that request. I'm asking you to do the same."

The sheriff blew out a breath. "Who made this request?"

"That's not important. The Governor and I feel very strongly that nothing should be done to possibly endanger the family."

"A man's been killed, murdered. I have a responsibility to the people of this county to bring those who did it to justice."

"Do you have any proof that anyone's been killed?"

"I have an eyewitness report." Crap, he hated being on the defensive with this snake. He didn't have a body, all he had was a phone call. Damn.

"You have a responsibility to see that no harm comes to the Stevens family. Have I made myself clear?"

"Yes." The sheriff's voice had gone quiet, dangerously quiet to those who knew him well.

"Good night, Sheriff Thomasen. I'll check in with you tomorrow."

Zeke carefully replaced the receiver. He sat fuming and confused. What the Sam Hill was going on? Someone was pulling strings.

Those rat bastards in the state house. They didn't give a damn about a murder in his county. All they cared about was feathering their own nests. Power and money trumped everything else.

"God damn it," he growled. He needed to get up there. Nobody was going to get away with murder in his county. Sitting here was driving him nuts.

Chapter 14

Sally Carter walked into the office, saw the look on Zeke's face and started to back out.

"Hold it, Sally. Have you got something for me?"

"Yes, Sheriff, got a bunch."

This youngster was fast. The sheriff sat back and closed his eyes, nodded his head. "Anything you can tell me will be welcome."

"Okay, last thing first. James Taylor is a lawyer in Wisconsin. Member of the state bar in good standing, partner in a law firm, bunch of certifications and awards. Owns some land in Flint County twenty miles south of town. Sixty one years old, divorced a couple of times. Want his educational background?"

"No, he seems to be what he claims to be, if he really is Taylor."

"I printed his photo from his law firm's web site." She handed the paper to him.

"Yep, that's him. What about Stevens?"

"Chet Stevens, Jr., resides in Boulder, Colorado. Also has houses in Palm Springs, California, and Coral Gables, Florida. Want to know what country clubs he belongs to?"

"I'll pass on that. Okay, he's got loads of money. Where does it come from?"

"That's where it gets interesting. Only thing I could find is he sits on the board of directors of West Slope Oil and Gas. Chet Stevens, Sr., is president and chairman of the board."

"West Slope sounds familiar."

"Yup, it owns West Slope Drilling. And West Slope Drilling owns the lease on Flat Top."

"Okay, this is starting to make sense. Anything else?"

"The company made a hundred million in profit last year according to SEC filings. Chet Stevens, Sr., is a prominent contributor to conservative politicians."

"How did they get the lease on Flat Top?"

"I don't know. Lease granted during the Bush administration, no record of any public hearing."

"Ah." The sheriff nodded, his face thoughtful. He looked over at Sally. "This has helped a lot. Can you see if there is some connection with the Governor or the Attorney General?"

"Be happy to. This is fun for me."

After Sally left Zeke put his feet up on the desk. He stared into the darkening room. This had to be a kidnapping and somebody had a ton of clout. He had to get up there. The National Forest was huge, much of it wilderness. If whoever it was left the camp, they might never be found. Not on his watch, not in his county.

Chapter 15

He woke at first light, slumped next to the now dead fire, frozen stiff. Jim struggled to get up on his numb legs. He stomped around and flapped his arms to get his circulation going. His back was stiff and achy. It took a few minutes for him to be able to stand up straight. He wanted to relight the fire, but figured it wouldn't be a good idea in daylight. Someone could smell it or see the smoke. He'd just have to keep moving. The creak and crackle of his sixty year old joints told him that his body did not appreciate last night's accommodations.

Buck looked over at him and gave a low grumble, his "I'm hungry" noise. Jim poured out a pile of horse cubes and looked around. It was still snowing, the air cold but still. He guessed it to be about thirty degrees. He took a deep breath, smelled a mixture of wet pine needles, resin, and horse manure.

The horse would need to drink again. Best to do it now while it was still snowing to cover their tracks. He made a breakfast of the last of the pate and cheese, washed it down with a beer, hopping up and down for warmth while he ate. Felt somehow decadent. Wished for hot coffee while the horse finished the cubes.

They walked down the slope to the creek. There was about six to eight inches of snow. He knew there would be a lot more snow at higher elevations. No way would the kidnappers get near Florence Pass today. Bob would know this, too, but the flatlanders might not. It would probably be a couple of days before anyone could get up and through the pass. If they didn't know this they might well leave the camp. That might mean an opportunity for the sheriff to rescue Bob and the campers.

The creek was wild when they got to it. Yesterday it had sparkled as it splashed around the rocks. Today the rocks, even the biggest, were under water. The water shot along its channel, a solid flow, unbroken, like a liquid freight train, barely contained within its banks. Normally one to two feet deep, today it was almost four feet deep, dark, no bottom visible. It looked angry, foreboding. Anyone crossing on foot would be swept away. He shivered. Gone was the friendly gurgle of yesterday, the creek roared.

Jim found a cove where he and Buck could get at the water without stepping into the current. As he watered Buck, he looked around. Right along the edge of the cove he saw several stalks of Indian paintbrush, the red standing out against the snow, and purple bits of lupine bent over. There were moose prints in the mud and small trout in the still water.

He took a drink. The water was so cold it was barely liquid. As far as he could see up and down the creek, the shrubs and trees near the banks were weighed down by the wet and heavy snow. Thick white on top and deep green on the bottom, the pine boughs were just barely above the torrent. Flat flakes of snow were falling slowly into the dark water, melting, dissolving, and swept away. He sighed, taking in the cold, damp smell of wet snow. He was glad he hadn't restarted the fire. In the crisp air the smell would carry.

"Well, Buck, I think it's time for us to do a little scouting. Let's go saddle up."

Shortly Jim and Buck were picking their way quietly and slowly along the game trail that paralleled the main trail. When they got even with the camp, Jim pulled out the binoculars and studied the hill where the camp was. The light was dim under the snow clouds, fat flakes filled the air between him and the camp, blurring his view and adding to the sense of distance, like looking through a tunnel.

There was smoke from the cook tent. On any other day that would be Bob making breakfast. Someone was chopping wood. "Buck, I bet they had the wood stove going all night. They slept warm and toasty. They're going to have a surprise when they see the creek. It's risen by at least two feet already and will get higher and faster as the snow starts to melt."

Buck grunted as he looked at the creek. Jim doubted the killers would get their ATVs across the creek. It would be several days before the water would go down to where it had been yesterday. This narrowed the options for the killers even more. They would either have to hole up until the creek went down or go out on horseback.

About a half an hour later the snow had stopped. Jim saw several figures at the top of the hill in front of the camp. He could see them gesturing toward the creek. The big bald bastard was shaking his fist. It looked like a pretty heated discussion. Somebody brought Bob up there. The big guy got in Bob's face. Then the men went back toward the camp.

He hoped they would hole up at the camp and wait for the creek to go down. If they stayed put, then it would be easy for the sheriff to trap them. If they left, the sheriff would have a tougher time. But either way he would be out of this and go down to the trailhead. He'd be off the hook, could pass off all responsibility, let the professionals take over.

He wondered when the sheriff would finally show up.

Chapter 16

Big Jack and Botts and their crew stood at the top of the hill and looked down at the creek. It was deep, fast, and roaring.

One of the men, Larry, spoke. "No way we can get through that with the four wheelers. We'll have to wait for the water to go down."

Jack snarled, "No, we'll wade it if we have to. Go get that guide. Bring him here."

"Damn mountains, damn weather, damn creek. Stupid word, creek. It's a fucking flood. I'm starting to hate this place and everything about it. First the rain and cold, then snow. Christ, it's summer. How can it snow in the damn summer? Now this flood."

He stood there in the snow at the top of the hill. The whole world around him was white, everything but the raging water at the foot of the hill. A breeze from behind made him shiver and brought the scent of wood smoke and manure. The moving air shook snow off pine boughs next to him.

Jack spat and glared at the scenery. He'd been hired to do this thing. The payoff would make him rich, he'd be set for life. Maybe he'd cut Stevens out, take it all. He'd think about that. Right now he had to get away from this spot, far away. He would make this thing work. Nothing and nobody was going to stop him.

Larry brought Bob up to the group, his hands tied behind his back.

Jack walked up close, stood a foot away, stared in Bob's face.

"You, guide, can horses get across the creek?"

Bob was ready for this. He knew the creek would be wild after all the rain. He had guessed why they had brought him up the hill. He figured they couldn't use their four wheelers. Horses could get across, but there weren't enough horses for these men and all the campers. Here was a chance to get these bastards away from the campers.

He nodded. "Yep, I'll get you and your crew across if you leave this family here unharmed."

Jack grabbed his shirt, pulled him close. "I don't make deals. Do this or I'll fucking kill you."

Bob, face hard, impassive, nodded.

Another guy, Fritz, turned to Jack. "None of us has ever ridden horses. Tiny and me grew up in Detroit. The other guys are city guys, too."

"You never been on a horse?"

"Nope, what for? We got four wheelers, don't need horses."

"Well, you need them today. Go help the guide with the horses. Put all our gear on the mules."

After the guide, Larry, and Fritz left, Big Jack turned to one of the other men. "Get back in the tent and make sure the women and children are tied good and tight. I don't want them getting loose. I want them stuck here for the cops to deal with, slow them down. If we hurry up the cops won't know that we've left and they might stake out the camp, buy us more time. That won't happen if they get loose."

"But, but, they'll die in that tent if no one finds them," the man stammered.

"Fuck if I care."

"Make sure Chet and the guide don't know. If they ask, tell 'em you were giving them water." Jack grabbed the man's coat. "Do a good job of it, I'm going to check on your work."

The man nodded reluctantly and walked off toward the cook tent.

Chapter 17

As Jim and Buck watched the camp the sun came out. Where sunlight hit the snow the reflection was blinding. Jim backed Buck up to keep them well in the shadows. The sky had gone from pearly gray to a rich cornflower blue. Within minutes the snow, already wet and heavy, started to turn to slush where the direct light hit it. In the shadows where they hid, the chill lingered unabated and their breath steamed.

While they waited, Jim tried not to think about what had been done to Bob and the camper family. He had heard no gunshots, but that didn't reassure him. If they were alive, they were surely in rough shape. They would have spent the night in fear and uncertainty about whether they would live. The kids must be terrified.

He thought back to winter trail rides. Snow deep in the woods, the trees stark and bare, asleep. Loping on snowmobile trails, flying across empty fields, not a care in the world. And after, Buck snug in his stall and hot coffee in the house. That seemed like another lifetime.

Jim realized that he felt different today. Even though he'd had a crappy night's sleep, he felt confident and strong. He was ready. He wasn't afraid. Soon he would know what the flatlanders were going to do, stay or go. He'd call the sheriff, his assignment done.

He was thinking about a hot shower and breakfast when men on horses appeared at the top of the hill. Jim did a count – eight horses and three mules. Jim recognized Bob who was leading the three mules on a pack line. The bastards were riding out and they had Chet with them. Jim backed Buck down behind the ridge to wait and see which way they would go. He was relieved that something was happening. He was tired of waiting. Where the hell was the sheriff?

The group rode down to the creek, Bob in the lead. The horses pranced a little when they got near the rushing water, nervous, goosey. The riders were looking at the creek then looking at each other, then back at the creek. Bob was first into the water.

With the creek this high and fast, crossing it even on horseback was a challenge. The water was belly high on Bob's horse. His boots and pants were getting soaked. It was slow going as the horse and mules picked their way over rocks in the swift current.

"Buck, let's see how these guys do crossing the creek. They don't look too happy on the horses. Maybe they'll do something stupid." Sure enough, the first of the men to try to cross the creek made the mistake of kicking his horse to hurry it across. The horse stumbled and the guy fell off. The current carried him several hundred feet before he could grab a low branch and pull himself out.

Jim chuckled. "Buck, this guy is going to freeze his ass in no time. Plus he lost the long gun he was carrying. This guy will be useless in an hour."

There was much shouting down at the creek and several guns were pointed at Bob. Jim could see Bob was shouting back at them, probably telling them to just let their horses pick their way across the creek at their own speed. And indeed that apparently was the advice and the remaining men and Chet Stevens crossed the creek without further mishap.

The men looked perched atop the horses, clearly novices. Most had a death grip on their saddle horns and no slack in the reins. Some were crouched forward in the saddle, others leaning way back. All looked unhappy and uncomfortable. The horses pranced about, reacting to conflicting messages from their riders. Although accustomed to inexperienced riders, they were not happy about how their mouths were yanked by the nervous men.

"Buck, look how these guys are sitting. I don't think they've ever been on a horse before. That's another edge for Bob and maybe for the sheriff, too."

Buck watched the horses and riders with interest. He gave a gentle snort when the man fell into the creek. Jim shushed him and Buck shook his head. A human falling off a horse was not something he saw often and it seemed to amuse him.

Buck muttered – huh, huh, huh – as the horses were yanked around by the nervous men. He could see the looks in the horses' eyes, wide open with the whites showing. Heads held high, noses pointed almost straight up, tails cranked to the side, all clear signs to Buck that the horses were very unhappy. Pissed off was what they were, although "pissed off" is not an expression thought by horses. He could tell that the horses wanted to dump the men but had been trained to put up with idiot greenhorns. If a horse could feel sympathy, Buck felt it.

Bob was disappointed that the guy who fell off his horse managed to pull himself from the creek. He'd hoped the guy would be swept away. Oh well, that guy wouldn't be much use, soaked to the skin in this cold.

The big one, Jack, told him they were going to the pass. Bob knew that there would be a lot more snow toward the pass. The pass was at a much higher elevation, the rain would have turned to snow much earlier. The snow would be a lot deeper and drifted, impossible to get through to the pass. He wasn't about to tell him that. He wanted these bastards away from the camp, away from the campers. When the snow stopped them he'd have to figure something to offer them or face the consequences.

Chapter 18

Everyone had now gathered on the trail. The guy who had taken the ice cold bath struggled to get back on his horse. Jim was pretty sure that none of them was eager to re-cross the creek to go back to the camp; that would be their last resort. Good.

With Bob and the string of mules leading, the group headed up trail toward the pass. Jim watched them slowly move off. He knew the trail well. The first couple of miles or so would be relatively easy going as the trail was flat and under tree cover. The snow would not get seriously deep until they got past Medicine Cabin Park and started the steep climb away from the creek and got near the tree line.

Jim understood that Bob had deliberately not warned the flatlanders about what to expect toward the pass. He was leading them away from the campers. The men might shoot him if they decided that he had misled them on purpose. That was Bob, he'd risk his life to protect his campers.

Now what? Where was that fricking sheriff? Jim rode Buck back to the base of the ridge and tied him to a big pine.

"Buck, I'm going to climb up and call the sheriff. I'll be back."

He left his duster and chaps with the horse. That made the climb a little easier. He called the sheriff from the same spot as the night before.

The sheriff answered immediately. "Zeke Thomasen."

"Sheriff, Jim Taylor. Where the hell are you? They've left camp and are heading up toward Florence Pass."

"Slow down, Jim. Who left?"

"The flatlanders with guns and they've got Bob and Chet Stevens." Jim paused, willed himself to slow down. "The creek's way high. They had to leave their ATVs. They're on horseback."

"What about the rest of the family?"

"Didn't ride out, still in camp. Don't know what shape they're in." He was tapping his foot. "Where are you?"

"Okay, Jim. Settle down. I've had some problems. I'm still in town."

"What?" Jim screamed in the phone.

"Calm down and listen. I'm trying to get some help so I can get up there. Damn politicians are sticking their noses in. They've tied my hands. I'm not giving up. Now listen."

Jim took a deep breath and blew it out. "Okay, I'm calm. Go on." I can't believe this. Oh, man.

"I think this is a kidnapping. I need you to be my eyes and ears. You've got to keep track of where those bastards are and let me know. If they slip away we'll never find them. Do you think you can do that?"

Jim shook his head, looked up at the sky. "You've got to be kidding. Look, Sheriff, I'm just a tired old lawyer. I've never been in anything like this." Jim paused and thought a bit. "They went up the trail toward the pass. We had a lot of snow last night. I'm certain they'll never get to the pass. What

60

about the people in the camp? When those guys get turned back they could go back to camp. So what do I do about the kids and the women?"

Zeke hesitated, he wanted the killer but there was the family to consider. "You've got to tail them a ways then check on the camp. You don't want them to turn back right away and catch you at camp. You'll have to figure something to do with them, hide the campers or something."

Jim groaned. "Or something? Jesus, Sheriff, you don't ask much, do you? I guess I don't have much choice. I'll do whatever I can. Just get your ass up here."

"Believe me, Jim, I'm trying my best."

Chapter 19

Jim scrambled back down to Buck and mounted up. He was breathing hard, trying to comprehend the situation. Innocents stranded at the camp. Kidnappers on the trail and they were going to come back this way sooner or later. No sheriff. No posse. It all came down to him and Buck.

This was totally, fucking nuts. "Fuck me and the horse I rode in on."

Buck stopped and turned to look at Jim.

"Sorry, sorry. It's not fair. This whole mess up here and the sheriff just told me to figure it out for myself." He took a deep breath. Easy, Jim, save the attitude. You've got to do this and do it right. The sheriff is a no show. The campers need you. And Bob and Chet. Don't fuck up.

Jim was anxious to check on the campers, but worried that the killers might backtrack and find him at the camp. The sheriff was right about that. "Buck, we'll tail them a ways. Make sure they get as far as that side trail to Powell Lakes. Then we'll scoot back here and check the campers. That should give us enough time even if they turn back at that point."

Jim squeezed his calves and Buck started up the trail.

Within a minute they passed the outlet from Deer Lake. Jim looked over remembering that Dave had been left where he fell. He saw a body sized hump in the snow, reckoned that must be Dave. No, he thought, it wasn't Dave any longer. It was Not Dave, a corpse. He shuddered.

For the next hour, Jim and Buck tailed the killers. They didn't need to see them. The killers were making enough noise that Jim could just follow his ears. Shouts and curses from the men carried in the still air under the trees. "This fucking horse won't mind me." "Shit, my ass hurts." "How much longer to this pass?"

This trail was one of Jim's favorite rides in the Big Horns. It started at the Archer Corral trail head and then followed the valley in which the north fork of Clear Creek ran. It went upwards in fits and starts for almost fifteen miles going through open parks and deep pine woods.

The trail was wide in most places below the wilderness boundary. The views from the trail were of pine covered ridges, only the very tops of the massive, rocky mountain peaks visible. In other places one could see huge boulders and jagged rock outcrops. Tiny streams cut across the trail, bordered by wildflowers. Once past that boundary, the trail narrowed considerably and was mostly under the trees until it got to the tree line. Past the tree line it rose steeply and clung to the north rim of the valley that the creek had created. At this part of the trail the massive mountains could be seen in their full majesty, many extending about 12,000 feet. The tallest peaks always sported at least patches of snow. The mountains closest to the trail presented sheer cliffs topped by cirques and arêtes. The cliff walls dripped with melt water which fed the creek.

Eventually the trail narrowed to where it was barely wide enough for one horse. Here the trail got dicey with a drop off of a steep five hundred feet on one side and a sheer cliff up on the other side. Even in good weather that part of the trail was intimidating. One had to trust his horse, remember that the horse didn't want to fall off the edge either. Then suddenly the trail broadened out at Florence Pass. At Florence Pass was the eponymous Florence Lake which held some sizeable trout. What did they want at the pass? Not fish.

Also at the pass, to the north, was Bomber Mountain, so named for the wreck of a B-17 strewn over the summit. Jim always thought of those poor airmen who had died at the top of the mountain, their remains found a year later. He made a mental note to remind the sheriff that Dave's body had been left at the lake. Anyway, the view from the summit of Bomber Mountain was awe inspiring. One could see the peaks of the Big Horns stretching all the way up to Montana to the north. To the west were the central arid barrens of Wyoming and then the Rocky Mountains. Several trails led off from Florence Pass. He bet they wanted one of those trails.

Jim knew that no one would see any of the higher reaches of the trail this day. He doubted that the group he was following would get much past the tree line. From Bob's camp to the pass, the trail gained about two thousand feet of elevation, topping off at over 10,000 feet. Snow often blocked the trail even into late July. Today there would be deep snow drifts, impassible even for horses. When the group got blocked by snow Bob would have to do some fast talking. Nothing he could do to help. Instead he pondered what to do with the campers. Hide them? Christ, Sheriff, that's nuts.

When the trail began to steepen, Jim figured they'd followed long enough. He knew he and Buck could get back to camp long before this group even if they turned back immediately.

He asked Buck for a lope and they raced back toward camp. Wind in his face, trees rushing past, flashes of sunlight, Jim gave himself over to the ride, caught up in the rhythm of the horse. It was a respite from worrying about Bob and the campers. He knew Bob would be all right as long as the killers needed him, but he'd been afraid of what he might find at the camp.

Chapter 20

They'd made it to the tree line. The last thousand yards had been a struggle, the snow deeper and the wind whipping hard, gritty snow into their faces. Clear of the last trees there was no shelter from the wind. They were in a world of blinding white, sunlight reflecting off the snow, all around them dazzling and painful. Cliffs and jagged peaks loomed in the distance. Ahead was a five foot snow drift across the trail blocking their progress. One rider tried to get his horse to go forward but the horse refused, ignoring his kicks and curses.

Bob shouted, "The horses can't get through this and it'll only get worse the higher we go."

Big Jack steered his horse next to the guide. "How much farther to the pass?"

"Another couple miles. The snow will only get deeper and there's no cover. It gets real narrow with a five hundred foot drop off. It can't be done, even on foot. No way!" I knew we'd get stopped by the snow. Now I've got to do some fast talking or they'll shoot me. I'll offer them the trail past Ant Hill. That will keep them away from camp and buy me some time.

The other riders gathered around. Tiny, who had fallen in the creek, was shivering and his teeth were chattering. All looked very haggard and jumpy, hunkered into their clothes to escape the wind.

Jack pulled a pistol from under his coat. "Guide, you knew this would happen. You've got to get us to the pass and then to Ten Sleep Lake trailhead lot day after tomorrow at the latest. I can't wait for the damn snow to melt."

Big Jack rammed the gun into Bob's cheek. Bob closed his eyes and waited for the shot he wouldn't hear. He'd known this was the risk of this gambit, had accepted the risk as the price for protecting the family back at camp. But he didn't want to die and was not ready to give up. He opened his mouth to speak.

Jack pulled the trigger. The boom reverberated off the surrounding cliffs.

Bob opened his eyes. He wasn't hit, wasn't dead. Then Jack was talking.

"The next one won't be in the air," he snarled. "Talk to me, guide, how are you going to get us through? You're a dead man. You set us up. Why shouldn't I shoot you?"

Bob raised his hands. "I didn't know what we'd find up here. I can't get you there until the snow melts. I can get you to another trailhead besides where you came from but we'll have to backtrack. Should get you there tomorrow if your crew can stay on their horses."

"They'll stay on their horses or I'll leave them up here to freeze to death. Okay, guide, we'll try this other way." Big Jack pointed his gun at Bob's head. "If you're lying to me, I will kill you."

Bob figured they'd kill him sooner or later. At least now he had some time to find a way to escape.

Chapter 21

At a lope, it took them only twenty minutes to get back down the trail to where they could cross the creek to the camp. The water seemed even higher and faster. Over the past fifteen years Jim had been to this camp, he had probably crossed the creek over a hundred times. Today the creek was worse than he'd ever seen. Even in the bright sunlight the water was dark, threatening, bottomless. The water rushed past, tearing downward, irresistible. He didn't fancy crossing this torrent, but the campers were on the other side. There was no choice.

The creek frightened him. Jim knew he had to swallow his fear. He had to trust Buck. Buck had forded the creek a dozen times already this week without a problem. Just go ahead and do it. Don't let Buck know how scared he was.

When they got to the edge, Buck paused. It was even deeper than when they'd had a drink hours before. He looked at the roaring water and snorted. He looked back at Jim.

"Yeah, we have to cross. The kids, Buck, they need us. You can do it."

There was a cold knot in his stomach. He mustn't let the

horse sense any hesitation. The campers were on the other side, there was no other way. He clucked to get Buck started.

Buck let out a huge snort and shook himself, then he waded into the torrent.

Within a second the water was up to Jim's knees. Buck was almost swimming. Jim could feel the water pushing the horse. Ice cold and implacable. He'd never forded anything this powerful before. He was helpless, just baggage. It was all up to Buck. He looked upstream. The creek was a black snake winding through a world of white. The roaring of the water filled his ears.

They hit a hole, Buck flailed with his fore feet and the current started to swing him. Jim held his breath, thought they might lose it, get swept away, go under, get smashed into a boulder. The water was up to Buck's withers. Jim was soaked up to his butt. The creek was a monster, a hungry monster ready to eat anything that entered it. It wanted them. It would carry them away.

He and Buck plus the saddle weighed well over half a ton and yet the water was lifting and pushing them. The pressure was incredible, like a hundred fire hoses blasting them from the side. Jim felt Buck's hind feet begin to scrabble for purchase on the rocky creek bed.

Jim looked downstream. He knew there were boulders hidden under the torrent. If the current swept Buck up they'd be thrown into those nasty rocks.

Then Buck gave out a big grunt and the horse gathered his hind quarters and lunged. He got all four hooves on the bottom again and plowed his way to the bank, his legs pumping in an underwater gallop. When they got to the bank Buck sprang up onto shore.

Buck charged up the hill to the camp, his powerful quarter horse rump propelling them. At the top Jim dismounted. His legs shook and he almost collapsed. He was soaked to the waist and ice cold. He steadied himself with a hand on the saddle. Jim reached up and hugged Buck's neck. Buck snorted, his nostrils flared from the exertion. Jim led him to the picket line under the trees and tied him with enough slack that he could munch on the horse cubes the other horses had left.

The cook tent was twenty yards away. Jim was afraid of what he might find inside. He approached cautiously. Would he find bodies?

Then he heard voices.

Chapter 22

Zeke hung up the phone. He chewed on his cheek as he replayed the conversation. The call had gotten him nowhere. The FBI special agent was polite but made no promises. The feds wouldn't call it a kidnapping without a ransom demand. They would check with the senior Stevens. Promised to call the sheriff back. Zeke disliked dealing with the FBI. They were arrogant and condescending. Calling them had been a last resort. The Attorney General had warned off the neighboring sheriffs. They were politicians now, just like the Attorney General. Ten years ago they'd have come to help no questions asked. He would just have to pull men from Flat Top and hope the protesters didn't notice. He'd have to tell the Forest Service to handle it without his help.

Damn, he needed a drink. Needed sleep more. He'd got maybe two hours last night. Looked at the photo of his wife, dead ten years now. Still missed Louise. He'd never considered finding someone else. Zeke had always been able to talk through things with her. She'd been his rock for thirty years. He knew he'd never find anyone who could take her place so he hadn't tried. Shook his head. Boy, he sure needed her now.

Sally Carter stuck her head in the door. "Got a minute, Sheriff?" This morning she sported a purple Goofy shirt.

"What have you got for me?"

"First thing this morning I got through to the corporations office in Delaware. That's where West Slope is incorporated. Had them email me 2009 annual report filed by the company. I think I found the Wyoming connection."

"Come on, Sally. Tell me."

"The report lists an ex-vice president of the United States as a consultant to the chairman of the board. Paid in stock options plus a cash fee."

"Our very own native son?"

"Bingo."

Damn politicians. Always meddling where they had no business. Didn't trust a one of them. Bought and paid for. Whores.

Chapter 23

"Oh, shit. They've come back. We're all going to be killed."

"Quiet, don't give them any reason, just be still and do whatever they tell us to do, we don't want to end up like Dave."

Jim opened the tent flap. The warmth almost knocked him over. He had been out in the cold so long.

"Hey, folks, I'm the cavalry to the rescue."

"Oh, god. You're Mr. Lundsten's assistant. Where have you been?"

"Ma'am, I've been waiting for those bastards to clear out. I saw them leave with Bob and your husband. I followed a ways." While he was talking, Jim had grabbed a big kitchen knife and had started cutting the bonds of the campers who were bound hand and foot.

"I saw them shoot Dave. Are the rest of you okay? Are you strong enough to move out?" Jim addressed this to the fortyish woman who was the mother of the two children in the party. Stella Stevens looked like a wreck. Her eyes were red rimmed with dark bags underneath. She had a split lip and an angry looking bruise on her cheek. Her hair was tangled and her clothes were ripped and filthy.

She sat with her children and their nanny. The boys were squirming, restless. They were filthy, but appeared to be unharmed. He reckoned they could handle a hike, probably be good for the boys.

The woman looked around at her boys. "I think we're fine physically, but Chet, my husband…I don't know, they saw him dragged from here. They saw Dave killed." She paused, eyes tearing up. "And that big bastard hit me." She appeared more in shock than the children.

"Ma'am, I've got to get all of you out of here as quick as we can. I'm afraid the killers will be back. They headed up toward the pass. Pretty soon they'll find that the snow is too deep up there and they'll come back here to hole up again."

"How will we get out? We heard them talking about how high the creek was and they took all the horses." She was wringing her hands repetitively and sounded close to hysterical.

"I know. You can't go that way. Besides, they might come upon you on the trail even if you did get across the creek. You're going to have to hike out another way. I want you and Eve to put on your warmest clothes, do the same with the boys. Grab some backpacks and stick dry clothes and food in them. You've got to get this organized and fast."

It looked like everyone's belongings had been piled right outside the cook tent under the outdoor dining table. Eve had grabbed packs and was stuffing them quickly. Stella Stevens seemed stunned and was just sitting on the floor of the tent.

"Eve, you've got to get Stella moving, we don't have much time. Does anyone have a cell phone?"

"I do," Eve said, "but it doesn't work here."

"I know, but it will work where you're going."

"Where are we going?" she asked. She looked to be about twenty, tall and athletic looking, blond hair in a pony tail. She seemed determined and calm. He hadn't really interacted with her before, she was always busy with the kids. Jim decided to put her in charge as Stella appeared to be useless.

"Eve, you're going to have to lead the family out of here. Can you read a map?"

"Yes, but what about you?"

"I'm going to get you started and then I'm going to try to help Bob and Chet, follow them." Jim pulled a topographic map out of one of the boxes under the cook stove and spread it out on the table. "Here, I'll show you. Here is the creek and here is the camp. See these lines all close together? That's the ridge behind the camp. The top of that ridge is about five hundred feet higher than the camp. From the top of the ridge you'll see a bunch of lakes. They're called the Seven Brothers. It's possible that there are people camped by one of those lakes; they're pretty popular this time of year. Best of all, your cell phone will work at the top of the ridge. I'm sure the sheriff will have people come for you."

Eve took all of this in. Jim sensed that she would pull it off. The kids were dressed in parkas with little packs on their backs. They seemed eager to get away from the camp.

Jim grabbed the woman by the shoulders and lifted her to her feet. "Ma'am, you've got to go now. You've got to get your kids out of here. In an hour you'll be at the top of the ridge and you can call for rescue. They'll probably send a chopper."

The young kids picked up on this. "Come on, mommy. Let's get a helicopter ride!"

Mrs. Stevens moved like a zombie, face expressionless,

limbs stiff. Eve got her into a parka and got her moving. Took an arm and guided her.

Jim escorted them through the trees. About a quarter mile from the cook tent, they came to the base of the ridge. It was a steep climb, but doable. The slope was close to forty five degrees but rocks and trees provided lots of handholds and places to rest. The snow would make it more difficult but the climb would be worse after the snow melted and made everything muddy. It would take Eve a while to get Stella to the top, but the possible return of the killers would provide ample motivation.

Jim shook Stella's shoulder. "You can do this. I've done it and I'm a lot older than you. Just use the trees and shrubs as handholds."

Jim took Eve aside. "When you see the sheriff tell him what I'm doing. I'll follow those guys and when I'm sure I know where they're going, I'll call him."

She looked him in the eye and nodded. "Thanks for coming for us." Eve smiled. "Be careful."

Jim smiled back. "Always."

The family started up, Eve helping Stella and the boys, happy to be moving, ranging ahead. Jim grinned as he pictured Eve's smile. Wished he was thirty years younger. Heard the Dead singing 'Good morning little school girl, can I come home with you?' Shook his head. "Stop that, you old fool."

Jim watched for several minutes and then went back to camp, relieved of worry about the camper family. Now he focused on his friend Bob and Chet. He knew he couldn't quit, had to follow through with what the sheriff needed.

Jim ransacked the camp for anything useful. He grabbed two backpacks. He stuffed one with any ready to eat food:

apples, a can of mixed nuts, snack bars, a jar of peanut butter, and lots of candy bars. He ate a few candy bars as he searched, he was starving. He found a coil of rope, a hatchet, a boning knife and sheath, a box of matches. He stowed these in the second pack.

He found his own duffel bag and dug out dry clothes. Jim sat down and pulled off his soaked pants and socks. The warmth of the tent felt great but he knew he couldn't linger. He pulled his wet boots back on, The dry socks wouldn't be dry for long so he grabbed another pair to pack.

He hurried through his search, afraid that the kidnappers would catch him here. He knew that they would not want to cross the creek again, but the camp offered a warm and dry place to hole up to wait for the snow to melt. He added a flask of scotch whiskey to his pack and quickly left the tent.

He went to the picket line. Jim hooked the packs over the saddle horn, one on each side. He took Buck's reins and walked him to the top of the hill. He got the binoculars out and scanned across the creek. No sign of Bob and the others. He looked up toward the pass. Everything was covered with a blanket of snow, dazzlingly white in the sun. Even looking up at the sky hurt his eyes, the reflection from the snow almost blinding.

They had to re-cross the creek. Jim really didn't want to ford it again as the last time they were almost swept away. Fording again would be tempting fate. And he didn't want to be caught in the middle of the creek if the killers came back.

He'd try to find a place where they could jump the creek. Jim had never asked Buck to jump, but he remembered someone once telling him that all horses could jump if they had to. He was about to find out.

Jim blew out a breath and swung up into the saddle. They rode down to the creek. He scanned up and down for a likely place. They needed the creek to be narrow and a flat approach to gain speed for the jump. Falling short on the jump was not an option. Not for the first time, Jim realized that his past despair seemed insignificant compared to his present reality.

A few hundred yards down stream, the creek narrowed to where the banks were much steeper. Jim had fished there in the past. The creek was only about six feet wide there, but today it was very deep. This was not a place to ford. A horse would be swept away in this high water. They walked up near the edge. The banks on both sides were grassy. Bob never crossed here because most of his campers were not experienced horse riders, but the jump could be done.

They both looked down at the surging water. Buck snorted and looked back at Jim. His eye seemed to say "Are you sure about this?" Jim stroked Buck's neck and reached behind and patted the horse's rump. "You can do this."

Jim rode Buck about thirty feet back from the edge. "All set old man? Let's us two old guys do it." He gave Buck a solid squeeze with both legs and Buck sprang forward into a bouncy lope. The moment of truth would come when they got near the edge. Buck would either jump or not. He'd have to be ready or get tossed into the creek if Buck refused the jump.

Jim hadn't jumped much. He'd had some spills, gone over a horse's head once when she refused a jump at the last second. Then she'd jumped, landed on him. He'd retired from jumping at that point, but knew the proper technique.

They picked up speed quickly. The edge of the creek came up. Oh shit, the water had probably undercut the bank. "Buck, now!"

Buck jumped.

Jim crouched forward in the saddle. He didn't look down, just straight ahead and held his breath. For a long moment he heard nothing, not even the roar of the creek.

They landed with a jolt on the far side of the creek with a foot or so to spare. Jim breathed. He heard the creek again. "Yeeha," he shouted, ignoring the need for stealth. He reached down and patted Buck on the neck. "Good job, you're the best. Might call you Pegasus. Let's go find Bob."

Chapter 24

They walked along the creek until they found an easy slope up to the trail. Jim turned Buck toward the pass. The cover of the trees gave them respite from the glare of the sun on the snow. The pine boughs were still heavily laden with snow. The vibration from their passing shook some boughs enough to cause them to dump their loads of snow. Both man and horse were hit from time to time by these mini avalanches.

After about a quarter mile, Jim stopped to listen. He heard nothing but decided they had best get off the trail before they met up with Bob and the kidnappers. He turned Buck up the slope on the far side of the trail and got them on top of a slight ridge and still under the trees.

Buck found the game trail. There were fresh tracks that Jim guessed to be mule deer. They followed this and were able to keep the main trail in sight and stay in the shadows. Jim dug into the candy bars. He had forgotten how hungry he was. The sun was heating things up and the snow would soon be soupy.

As they plodded along, Jim worried about Bob and Chet. Sooner or later the killers would be cornered by the sheriff or would run into a search party. When that happened, they could become casualties. Even if Stevens was being held for ransom like the sheriff believed, that wouldn't protect him in a shootout. Stevens might be an asshole, but Bob and Jim were responsible for his safety on the pack trip. And then there was Bob.

Bob and Jim had been friends for over twenty years, ever since Jim had taken his first pack trip with Bob. Bob was a self-described boy scout with a college education. He loved and respected the wilderness and wildlife. He took good care of his horses and mules and would not tolerate campers who might abuse the animals. Bob was about a half a dozen years younger than Jim. Medium height, he was barrel chested. His waistline had grown over the years and his face was proof of many trips in the mountains in all seasons. He was tough and despite his years and substantial belly, he could out hike all but the most athletic campers.

Jim and Bob shared a love of the Big Horns. Most visitors merely passed through on their way to the Tetons or to Yellowstone Park. This was fine with Jim. The Cloud Peak Wilderness within the Big Horns was accessible to hikers and horses without requiring the "technical skills" that the more rugged Rockies demanded and wasn't mobbed with visitors.

After going along for about half an hour, they came upon a meadow on the far side of the ridge, hidden from the trail. Jim tied Buck on a long line so that he could graze while he hid at the top of the ridge to watch the trail up ahead. "Just dig through the snow like you do back home."

Jim looked off to the south across the valley. All the rocky peaks were completely covered with new snow. High altitude wind sent plumes of white blowing off the crests, streaking in the bruised blue sky. Towering above the creek valley, the nearest rock face was practically vertical and presented an almost seamless wall a thousand feet up from the creek. Melt water made shiny streaks on the rock. At the top of the cliff, tiny waterfalls cascaded off only to disappear into mist part way to the valley floor.

He was sure that they would come back down the trail. There was no way they could get up to the pass and no decent place to camp anywhere higher up. It was already midday and with the snow turning soupy, it would be hard to find a dry place to camp until they got down well below the tree line.

The men were clearly not horsemen. Their asses would be sore by now, but he reckoned they would keep moving. They had left the comfort of camp. There must be some place they needed to be. If the sheriff was right about this being a kidnapping, maybe they were going to where they would get the ransom. They had abandoned their ATVs to keep moving upward. When they found their way blocked by snow, they would have to turn around. Going back to Bob's camp would be tempting; it was warm and dry and hidden from the trail. It could be easily defended.

The creek presented a tough problem, though. They had barely made it across before and it was still getting higher and faster. If they chose that option, they might well abandon the horses and cut down a big tree for a foot bridge. They had left their ATVs at the camp, but those were useless until the creek went down. They would lose freedom of movement if they chose the camp. Camp was easily defended but it also could be surrounded. Camp was a potential trap.

If they chose Bob's camp, what would they do about

Bob? Would they feel that they still needed him? If not, they would surely kill him. For all they knew, they still had potential hostages at the camp so if they chose to hole up at the camp, they might deem Bob surplus. And what would they do if they did get to camp? The family would be gone. They'd probably blame Bob for that, taking them on a wild goose chase up toward the snowed in pass. Then what? He shook his head. Jim realized he couldn't figure what these kidnappers would choose to do.

Bob has to be thinking along these lines too, Jim thought. To save himself and protect the campers he'll come up with another option for them, one that leaves them freedom of movement. What could he offer them? Jim pondered that for a minute. Another way out of the mountains. The pass was blocked and they'd for sure not want to go back to Archer trailhead. That's where any pursuit would start from. Bob could offer them another trail that would get them out to a different trailhead. That way he protects the campers and keeps himself useful to his captors.

Half way to Archer trailhead there was a park, a large treeless open area. There was a trail leading north from the park which would take them up a long steep slope along Ant Hill Mountain. Beyond Ant Hill, that trail would take them down from the wilderness and out on the plains north of town.

If I were Bob, that's what I'd offer them. They would have to camp somewhere tonight but they could make it out of the mountains late tomorrow. It would be a smart choice for the kidnappers; they would believe it gave them an element of surprise on the sheriff since only someone who knew the mountains would know that route. Jim walked back to Buck. "Buck, I don't think they'll go back to the camp. My best guess is they're too intimidated by the creek to want to brave it again if they have another option. I think Bob will take them through Soldier Park and up around Ant Hill and past Gem Lake."

Buck looked at him and snorted, his grazing interrupted. Jim gathered up the lead rope and swung into the saddle. "I figure we've got to stay ahead of them and do whatever we can until the sheriff can get here."

Jim guided Buck down to the trail and then nudged him into a lope. Buck's lope was smooth, seemingly effortless, like skipping downhill. But it was fast, their movement bringing fresh, brisk air against Jim's face. He loved the lope, could feel Buck's power, the flow of his muscle, and match his balance to Buck's motion, be one with the horse. They floated down the trail under the pine trees, dappled with sunshine. The creek roared along on their right. Resisting the urge to lope all the way to the trailhead, Jim brought them to a halt where they had spent the night. He wanted to salvage some of what they had left there.

He dismounted and led Buck up the slope. He picked up the panniers the mule had carried. Jim dumped some of the alfalfa cubes in one. He put the tarp and the back packs in the other. He decided to keep the load light for Buck and he'd walk for a while to give the horse a break. He tied the panniers together and draped them over the saddle.

Buck blew a raspberry. "Yeah, I know you're not a pack mule. Just remember you've got your supper on board. You're just going to have to 'cowboy up.'"

As they started off, Jim thought about what a ridiculous situation he was in. What was he doing lurking around the wilderness trying to outsmart a bunch of kidnappers? He'd rescued the campers. Now he should ride down and get help. Just get moving lickety split, get away before he got killed.

Screw the sheriff. This was the sheriff's job. But he couldn't abandon Bob. He had been a true friend for years. Bob had taken care of him and his family up here. Helped them have great times, kept his children safe in the wild when they were young. He couldn't live with knowing he'd left Bob up here like this. He'd stick with this until the sheriff showed up. He'd do what he could to get Bob out of this alive. He would not leave Bob in the lurch.

Jim sighed. "Well, Buck, a crazy man once said, 'When the going gets weird, the weird turn pro.' I guess I have just turned pro."

Buck snorted, whether in agreement or derision, Jim couldn't tell.

Jim realized that he had changed. He'd been in a near constant state of fear and desperation, anxious to leave and find a place of safety. Yet when he was at the camp he'd loaded up on what supplies and gear Buck could carry. He'd subconsciously been planning for the long haul. Now he was committed to doing whatever he could to help Bob. "Huh, turn pro indeed, old fool more likely."

He had no experience in law enforcement other than two summers in a district attorney's office during law school. That was hardly preparation for this. He did know the wilderness and he had the element of surprise. He figured he was grounded enough that he wouldn't convince himself that he was indestructible. He was a scrawny sixty year old, not a Rambo.

He was a trial lawyer, dealing with other people's problems day in and day out. While often interesting and engaging, the demands of his clients and his opponents frequently soured him on humanity. He would rather spend his time with horses. But he had become an expert at strategy and tactics, anticipating what the other side would do and preparing countermoves. He would have to outthink these kidnappers or whatever they were and use their weaknesses to his advantage.

Chapter 25

Deputy Davey Hopkins was the best tracker in the department. He turned away from the swirling pine needles as the helicopter took off. The bird turned and headed toward town. He hiked to the edge of the ridge that separated the Seven Brothers from the valley the campers had left.

He called in on a satellite phone.

"Sheriff, the chopper just left. I don't see any movement in the valley, just trees and lots of snow. It'll be easy to follow where these folks climbed up from Lundsten's camp. A kid could do it."

"Davey, remember we don't know who might be down there. Go slow. Call me when you get to the camp."

"Roger."

Davey Hopkins' descent was not stealthy. The wet snow had turned the ground to mud. He had to dig in his heels and half slide down the slope grabbing at any hand hold he could reach.

When he got to the bottom of the slope he stopped and listened for a few minutes. He heard nothing but the wind, water, and small animals. He crept to the picket line and stopped again. Still no sign of friend or foe. Finally he approached the tents. There was no sign of life and, thankfully, no bodies.

"Sheriff, I'm at the camp. No one here. I've found tracks. Older tracks, many horses and mules, leading from camp to the creek and another set, one horse, coming here and then back to the creek. My guess is that one guy jumped the creek."

"Jumped the creek?"

"Yep, I'm pretty sure."

"Can you get across the creek and track the big group?"

"No way. It's bad. I wouldn't try it even on a horse. And nobody's coming back over here. I'd guess it'll be days before anybody can cross."

"Any bodies?"

"Nope."

"You find any ATVs?"

"Six of 'em. Look fairly new."

"Okay, see if you can get serial numbers on the ATVs. Call when you get back up the ridge and I'll send the chopper for you."

"Roger."

Chapter 26

They went down the trail towards Soldier Park, Jim leading Buck. The snow was disappearing rapidly and with the gentle down slope the going was easy. The creek was now about a hundred feet below the trail but he could still hear it roaring. They passed a meadow where the creek meandered. There were several moose grazing by the creek apparently unconcerned about the torrent. Buck gave the moose the evil eye. He did not like moose.

Jim chuckled. "You know, Buck, you probably share an ancestor with those moose."

Buck snorted and walked on.

Jim realized that Bob had no idea he was stalking the kidnappers. He needed to leave Bob some kind of sign, something that would tell Bob that he was not alone, that someone was trying to help him. Bob would probably figure out who it was.

It had to be something that Bob would recognize but wouldn't tip off the others. Best to try several signs. Jim took the hatchet and chopped a blaze head high on a large pine tree right next to the trail. Then he chopped a blaze one foot below and a third one, one foot below that one. Nobody did blazes like that but those flatlanders wouldn't know that. Jim did this on several trees along the trail. Next, Jim cut several short pieces of rope. He tied these around trees that bordered the trail. If his captors noticed these, Bob could come up with some bullshit explanation.

They went through a section of trail that reminded Jim of a cathedral. The pine trees were seventy or more feet tall and blocked out most of the sunlight except over the trail. There was almost no brush under the trees. He had no sense of being closed in because the trunks were widely spaced. He could see fifty yards to either side. Riding along the trail seemed to him like going down the aisle in a huge church. The air was full of the crisp smell of pine resin and the musty aroma of wet pine needles. It was quiet, the only sounds were the muffled thumps of Buck's hoof beats on the thick carpet of pine needles.

A half a mile from the cathedral was a stretch where all the mature trees had been blown down many years ago. Huge trunks lay on the ground tangled with each other like a child's game of pickup sticks. Interspersed were young trees standing straight up taking advantage of the space their fallen parents had made. When the big trees went down their root balls came too, leaving circular holes in the ground and circles of earth, rocks, and roots tipped up vertically. The trail wound around the obstacles like a path through a giant's maze.

When Jim and Buck got to Soldier Park the snow was almost gone. The grass was wet and the park was deserted. He had hoped the park was empty, explaining the situation to campers and getting them to leave would not have been easy. The sun was getting low. It would be full dark in two hours.

They needed to get across the park and start up the Ant Hill trail but keep close enough to watch the group enter the park.

Jim led Buck under the trees on the west edge of the park and circled to the north. About half way around, they hit the Ant Hill trail. The trail went steeply up hill for about a hundred yards and then leveled off in a thick grove of aspens. Jim tied Buck to an aspen and walked back to the crest of the hill to watch and wait. He found a fallen log to sit on and got comfortable.

This park was named Soldier Park because two cavalry troopers were buried there. The trail through the park went right past the graves, grassy mounds marked off by logs and wooden crosses. The troopers had been killed by Indians (Jim forgot which tribe) back in the 1870s. Standing by the graves, one could look west and see the whole valley all the way up to the pass. It was a lonely place to die, but a grand place to be buried.

He knew he'd taken a gamble anticipating that Bob would take the kidnappers up to Ant Hill and beyond. There was another side trail, one that would go to Seven Brothers. If they went that way it could be a disaster if they found the Stevens family up there waiting for rescue. He didn't think Bob would lead them that way because they would have to ford the creek to get to that trail. Nothing he could do about it.

As he waited, he wondered how the Stevens family had fared. He was confident that they would make it to the top of the ridge and get through on the cell phone. He thought a helicopter was unlikely. The sheriff would probably radio up to the nearest lodge to send a rescue party up on horseback.

Once he collected the family, the sheriff would know more about what had happened, but not the whereabouts of

Bob, Chet, and the kidnappers. It would take time to organize armed search parties and there was a lot of wilderness to cover. It could be days before anyone could get near them, if ever. In the meantime these bastards would probably be long gone. Jim understood why the sheriff needed him to spy.

What would he do if they didn't show up here? He'd have to back track and try to find some trace of them, something to help the sheriff. And what if they'd killed Bob when the snow stopped them? Even then they didn't have much choice but to come back down and camp somewhere. He'd have to find them in the dark. That would be tricky and dangerous. He hoped it wouldn't come to that.

Eyes closed and head down, Jim had nodded off. Voices caused him to jerk awake. He was instantly alert. The group had entered the park and stopped. Jim was pleased that he had guessed right about their route and relieved to see Bob. But he noted that the kidnappers didn't let Bob lead the party. Bob was under guard. They had him in the middle, well covered by their weapons so he couldn't break away to escape, which made rescuing him a whole lot tougher. They didn't appear as vigilant about Chet, no weapons pointed at him. Probably realized that Chet was a useless turkey. Except he was worth a ransom.

There was an old campsite near the entrance to the park. The party stopped there and everyone dismounted. The sun had just set. Jim was sure they would camp there for the night. He could see how stiff the men were from riding all day. Some of them would be real saddle sore, these guys were a lot bigger than the women and children whose saddles they were using. He had to chuckle. The ride would be even worse the next day on the steep switch back trail around Ant Hill.

Soon there was a fire going. Jim could see Bob staring toward where the Ant Hill trail began. "Yes, he knows. He'll be ready."

It was time for Jim to feed himself and Buck and try to get a few hours of sleep. Unless the kidnappers got sloppy there wouldn't be a chance to spring Bob loose at the park. The camp was too exposed. He'd have to head up the mountain and look for an opportunity. To get a head start on them meant starting off in the middle of the night. He needed to get some sleep first or he'd be useless.

After he fed Buck, Jim ate a cold meal leaning against the horse. He was exhausted but felt the need to talk.

"Buck, we've done well so far. The campers are out of danger. We're a step ahead of the kidnappers. But I'm worried about Bob. At some point they may not need him anymore, if that happens they'll probably kill him. If we could only bust Bob loose. Damn sheriff. If he doesn't come through soon we may have to do something. I don't know how yet, but we've got the edge – we're in front of them and they don't know we're here."

Jim gathered a big pile of pine needles for a bed. He snapped up his duster and lay down pulling the tarp over him. He looked up at the horse.

"I'm going to try to get a few hours of sleep. I'm too old for this sleeping rough but at least it's not raining."

He was exhausted from the day and the rotten night before. Sleep pulled hard at him, like the current in the creek, grabbing him up, carrying his consciousness away.

Buck stood next to him, slowly chewing feed cubes. His ears were pointed toward the park. He could smell a faint trace of smoke from the campfire.

The horse was relaxed. The day had been busy and he was happy to eat and rest. Buck sensed the change in his human's mood. No longer scared and unsure, the man was determined, confident. This reassured the horse and he was content to rest and await their next day's efforts.

It would be a very long day.

Chapter 27

They had straggled into Soldier Park. The crew was clearly saddle sore, leaning forward and shifting around on their saddles. The men could barely manage to dismount. One of them collapsed when his feet hit the ground. He lay there groaning until Jack kicked him. Once on the ground, the men staggered about bowlegged like drunks. Most were rubbing their sore butts and moaning like calves separated from their mothers.

Bob walked up to Big Jack. "I need some help with the horses and mules. We need to get the saddles off, get them water, and feed them. Going to need them to climb a mountain tomorrow."

"Show me the map first, then my men will help you."

Bob got a Forest Service map out of his saddle bag. "We're here – Soldier Park. The main trail goes down to the trailhead, Archer Mesa. Over there is a side trail. It goes up the side of Ant Hill Mountain. At the top, the trail will take us to Cloud Peak reservoir. From there a rough road goes down to Piney Creek trailhead twenty miles north of town. It's a steep climb and the animals can't do it today. If we leave in good time tomorrow, I'll get you there by afternoon."

Jack grunted. He really had no choice but to try this route. The plan was bollixed up but this new location should work. They'd make their calls tonight. If only they had something beside the damn horses.

"Okay, guide. You can have three men to help you."

He turned to his men. "You, Larry, take two others and help the guide. Fritz, keep a gun on him. Tiny, since you're so damn cold, you start a fire."

Bob sat by the fire and stared off toward Ant Hill. He finally had time to think. Those signs along the trail today meant that Jim was around here somewhere. He figured that Jim would have checked on the campers and freed them. But the signs along the trail had to be a message. He guessed Jim was going to shadow this group. Bob didn't know what Jim had in mind but he had better be ready if a chance came up to get away.

He didn't know whether Jim had got through to the sheriff. If the sheriff did catch up it would be messy. Right now he was better off without Zeke. Jim and his horse could sneak around, a posse couldn't.

Bob had heard the men using names in front of him. They had gotten sloppy, probably because they were exhausted by the riding and the cold. Good, exhausted men make mistakes and might give him a chance to get away. He didn't have a plan but he knew that if he tried to escape and failed, the leader, Big Jack they called him, would kill him. The man was more vicious than a hungry grizzly. The bastard had almost shot him when the way to the pass was blocked. Leading them up there had been a big risk, but it had gotten them away from Stella, Eve, and the kids.

Chet was another matter. He had to be the reason behind all this. Why else would they bring him along? Was this a kidnapping? The guy was rich and said he was connected with that drilling operation over at Flat Top. He'd keep his ears open.

Big Jack sat across the fire from the guide. The man was thinking. He was too smart by half. He'd try to escape and he couldn't allow that. He'd made the guide point out the route on the map and then kept the map himself. If he had to kill the man he could still get his crew to the reservoir and then down to the trailhead, with or without horses.

These men he and Botts had hired were useless around the horses. They couldn't saddle the creatures without help from the guide. Up on the horses, they were as uncomfortable as he was. They were soft, whining all the time. And they were stupid, couldn't find their ass with both hands. They'd never make it in his old unit, let alone as private contractors. He wondered if they could keep their mouths shut when the job was done.

Jack stood up and motioned Botts to join him. They walked off a few yards. Jack squatted and spread the map on the ground. Botts pulled out a small flashlight and got down next to him.

He pointed. "This reservoir will work as a drop point. It's flat and that road will make for a fast trip to the trailhead. Look, there's only two ways to get there, the way we come in and the road from the trailhead. We put Horvath at the trailhead so we'll know if anyone tries to follow the ransom."

Botts grunted. "Yeah. With Horvath down below we've

got it locked. Nobody can follow behind us without us knowing. Besides, no one knows where we are or how we're gonna to get to the drop point. There's a highway just a couple miles from the trailhead. A few hours and we'll be well away. Yeah, it works." He looked over at Jack. "Be good to be done with these horses."

"Okay. I'm going to make the calls tonight." Jack paused and looked over at the camp making sure no one was within earshot. "What about our crew? Can we trust them when this is done? Do we tie it off to be safe?"

Botts was silent for a minute, sucked on his teeth. He and Big Jack had seen a lot in their years together in the army and as contractors in the Mideast. Jack had saved his ass more than once. He missed working with good, well trained men. But things had gotten too hot after that fuck up on the road outside the Green Zone. They'd had to leave in a hurry. These kids were just muscle, no brains. "You're right. One of them will get drunk some night and talk big. Yup, tie it off."

"On the way down when we're done."

"Got it."

"Okay, get the phone. Time to set this up."

Dude Horvath had served with Jack and Botts, always their driver. He answered on the first ring. Jack gave him the location and the timing. "Get to that trailhead the day before and stake it out. Call me when the delivery goes up. If anybody's going to move in on us it'll be then. I'll call you when we've got the money and start down to you."

"You got it, Jack."

"Remember that other thing I mentioned?"

"Yeah."

"Do it."

Botts grabbed Chet Stevens and brought him over to Big Jack.

"Well, Chet, time to call your dad."

"What's the plan?" he whispered. "I thought we had to get over the pass to make this work. I left a company truck at the Ten Sleep Lake trailhead. How am I going to get back to town?"

"Not to worry. You can ride back with whoever brings the money."

"But how do I get my share?"

"I'll get it to you. Otherwise you'll rat me out. You've trusted me so far."

"Yeah, and you've murdered Dave," Chet whined. "Kidnapping and ransom could be kept under the radar, murder won't be."

"And I'm going to kill the guide, too. You're in this up to your neck. Time for you to earn your share. Now call the old man."

Chet hung his head and nodded.

The elder Stevens answered right away. "Chet?"

"Dad, it's me."

"Chet, Stella and the boys...."

Big Jack grabbed the phone. "Stevens, you heard your son. If you want to keep him alive, listen carefully. Get paper and pen. You have somebody go to this trailhead day after tomorrow," he gave the map coordinates. "There's a rough road going up from the trailhead. He's to start up the road at ten o'clock exactly. He'll be watched. Better give him an ATV so he can haul the money. He's to follow the road up until he gets to a reservoir. He stops there and we make the exchange. We'll check the money, so don't fuck with me. Any cops show up anywhere and Junior here dies. You got this, old man?"

"I'm trying to put the money together. I need another day."

"Don't fuck with me."

"Ten million in cash is not easy, the money has to come from all over the country."

Big Jack covered the mouthpiece. "Chet, does he have the cash on hand? Says he needs another day."

Chet nodded. "Everything's electronic now. That much cash would be hard to get."

"Why didn't you tell me this before?"

"We had a plan that worked before. It gave him plenty of time. I think he's on the level."

"Okay, you've got an extra day. Everything else stays the same. No more delays or we kill Chet and disappear. Understand?"

"Yes. Let me speak with my son."

"Nope. You get to talk with him when this is over. Remember, I so much as smell a cop, your boy dies."

Big Jack hung up. "Okay, everything's in motion. I'll call Horvath with the new date. Time for chow and sleep."

He was satisfied with the plan. Chet was a weak link, but too gutless to disobey him. As for the guide, he'd keep him under guard. He looked around the campsite. The darkness was total. The fire was a comfort and would keep the guards awake, but he felt vulnerable for it made him an easy target. He reminded himself that there was no one near, they were miles from any other human. He'd post a two man guard anyway.

Chapter 28

The helicopter settled onto the baseball diamond behind the Sheriff Office. The slowing rotors stirred up dust from the infield, tornados of grit which collapsed when the blades stopped. He'd had Art Gonzales fly up to Seven Brothers to retrieve the four escapees. Zeke had not contacted the Attorney General or anyone else when he'd taken the call from Eve Larsson, the Stevens' nanny. He wanted first crack at interviewing the women.

The late afternoon sun was dulled by the haze from the evaporating moisture in the mountains, the sky a milky pale blue. He and Doris ushered the women and children into the lobby. He'd had Sally fetch sandwiches and drinks from Stockman's Diner on Main Street.

While Sally entertained the young boys with peanut butter and jelly sandwiches and computer games, he'd sat the women down in his office. He left the door open so they could watch the children. As they were settling in he opened a desk drawer and turned on a small tape recorder.

Stella Stevens was groggy, huge bags under her eyes, a tic in her cheek, and a general listlessness. She answered his questions in a monotone. The family was here because Chet was to monitor progress at the drilling site. The pack trip had been Chet's last minute idea. Dave Hammond, their assistant, worked for Chet's father. She didn't know his background.

Yes, the assistant, Jim, had cut their bonds. He'd sent them up that awful climb, abandoned them. He should have had the helicopter come to the camp. No, she didn't know where the men were taking Chet. They did mention a pass, it had a female name.

Chet told her they'd made him call his father, that they had made a ransom demand. He said he'd convinced them to take him and leave the family alone. She didn't see Dave killed, she had stayed in camp doing her nails. She wanted to call her father-in-law.

When he'd excused Stella to make her call, he focused on Eve. She'd been their nanny for two years. She was twenty two and from the Twin Cities, had met the family while in Colorado on a ski trip. She loved the boys, thought the parents were snobs but they treated her well and paid generously.

"I saw them shoot Dave. It was the bald one. There were six of them, two older, the others about my age. The older ones did all the talking. The bald one was in charge. He's big and nasty. He scared the shit out of me." She looked at the floor and gave a shudder. "The other one was short and had long hair. He looked at me like I didn't have any clothes on."

"Eve, tell me about Jim."

She smiled. "He was nice. He cut us free and sent us up that hill. He was polite and reassuring, but I could tell he was in a hurry. Jim said he had to follow the others, try to help." She thought for a few moments. "Jim said to tell you he'd call when he knew where they were going."

"Did Chet say anything about a phone call?"

"He said he'd called his father, something about money."

"Did any of the men say where they were going?"

"They didn't say. They were very upset when they learned about Jim not being in camp. I think that's why they left."

"Anything else you can tell me?"

"Well, there's one thing I thought was a little strange. It was Chet. He wasn't frightened like the rest of us. Pissed off about something, but not scared."

Chapter 29

Zeke stood looking at a map taped to the wall, hitting the palm of his hand with the other fist as he stared. Where were they? Where were they going? The Big Horn National Forest was huge, much of it trackless wilderness. Search and rescue was always a problem, but this was much worse because who they were seeking didn't want to be found. He had to narrow things down.

He knew where they had started, Bob Lundsten's camp, just off the Solitude Trail. They were on horseback. Mrs. Stevens said they mentioned a pass with a female name. That had to be Florence Pass. Jim believed that the snow had blocked the pass. Zeke hoped he was right; it would narrow the options some. If they made it to the pass they could easily disappear. At the pass trails led off in every direction. If the pass was closed, then the search area was smaller but still daunting.

Where was Jim Taylor? Was he even alive? Why hadn't he called in a report? His last call had the group going up toward the pass, but that was ten hours ago. Well, he was just a citizen, couldn't expect too much. He hoped the man didn't do something stupid and get himself killed. Bob Lundsten was also in the wind. They would have taken him along because of the horses. Their need of horses probably saved his life. They would need the horses or mules if they had anything to haul, like ransom.

He had two deputies freed up. He'd take them into the mountains in the morning if he could just narrow down the search. He'd called his contact with the FBI. The taped discussion of a ransom had done the trick. The agent promised to have a crew arrive in the morning. They would not be much help in the mountains, but they could block off trailheads. Maybe having the FBI here would shame the Attorney General into sending State Police. Same problem, where to send them.

Damn it all, where were they?

Chapter 30

Jim woke shivering in pitch darkness. He sat up, rubbed his face, and for a moment couldn't remember where he was. He heard heavy breathing next to him. Looking over, he could pick out a darker shape. It was big. He dug out his lighter and flicked it on. Buck was standing right next to him, eyes and ears pointed towards Soldier Park. And it all came back to him, murder, kidnapping, Bob a hostage, no damn sheriff. He gave a low groan. When would this be over?

Every bone, joint, and muscle ached. Sleeping in the cold on the hard ground was the pits. He was too old for this. He checked his watch – 2:47, no time for self pity, time to get his sorry ass moving. 'I'll sleep when I'm dead' ran through his head. "Yeah," he muttered, "but you are, Warren." Moving around would probably be better than lying on the ground anyway. He creaked to his feet.

"Thanks for taking the first watch, Buck," Jim whispered. He walked over and stroked the horse's neck. "I'll go have a look see. You wait here." The horse grunted.

Jim walked to the top of the hill, kind of feeling his way, careful not to make noise in the brush. Starlight lit the trail,

107

but he avoided it for fear of being seen. When he got to the crest of the hill he stood still and listened. Nothing. He crept forward until the camp was visible through the trees.

There was still a fire going and two of the kidnappers were sitting up by it. Stupid to try to sneak up on the camp, too much risk of someone hearing him or waking the horses and mules. He thought about freeing Bob. Something had to be done to help him. He was certain that they would kill him sooner or later. Where was the sheriff? Was he even in the mountains? The sheriff didn't know where they were. If anybody had the best chance of doing something for Bob, it was him, not the sheriff. There was no chance of doing anything here. Nothing for it but to head on up the trail. Staying ahead of them would give him the advantage; they would expect interference to come from behind.

Helping Bob sounded good, but how? He was outnumbered six to one and they were armed. If he did something stupid he'd be killed. He'd have to find a way, use surprise, take advantage of the terrain, maybe something to do with the horses. He knew the trail, was familiar with Ant Hill and the reservoir. He'd look for his chance.

He paused and shook his head. "Damn, I can't believe this. What I'm thinking? Geez Louise." Didn't want to over think the idea, better to just get moving. Jim shrugged and made his way back to Buck.

He fed Buck, groomed him, saddled him, and loaded him up again. "I'll walk with you, you've got enough to carry and the going will be steep." Buck gave a sigh and they started off.

For the first quarter mile, Jim stayed off the trail and led Buck under the trees where the pine needles muffled their footsteps. It was pitch dark under the trees and the going was slow. When they came to a steep down slope, Jim moved over to the trail. Here the stars provided ample light. The slope was so steep and rocky that he held onto Buck to keep from sliding on loose rocks. Jim hoped the hill would screen the clatter Buck's shoes made on the rocks. At the bottom there was a trickle of a stream. Both had a good drink.

When they were done, Jim stood still and listened. There was no hint of anyone following. All he heard was the soft gurgle of the water and the faintest whisper of a breeze in the trees. He checked Buck's load and stroked his neck. He stood for a minute gathering himself. The horse nudged him with his nose as if to get him moving.

The trail then crossed the meadow that Jim knew was called Triangle Park. The ground was soft and they moved silently. The glow from the moon and stars lit their way. The meadow shimmered, bright gray, surrounded by black forest. The wildflowers sparkled silver. The grass glistened with dew. The air was still, the meadow hushed. Jim smiled, the meadow was magical, straight out of a children's book.

"Hey, Buck, watch out for fairies. I swear they're watching us. Maybe they'll come out to dance."

Buck had never heard the word "fairies" before. He knew what "watch out" meant. His human did not sound worried, not at all. Buck kept a careful watch anyhow. He wanted to see what fairies looked like.

Once the trail left Triangle Park, it was hard work. The

climb was steady, almost two thousand feet higher in elevation to the top of the trail. In daylight, the scenery was beautiful, trees marching up the mountain side. As they left the park, the trees closed in on both sides, tall pines and spindly aspens. Very little light reached the narrow trail, but Jim's eyes adjusted to the dimness. It was like he was tunneling up the mountain.

The first stretch of trail was a steep uphill grade, fairly straight. After about a half a mile of steady climbing, they came to the first switchback. It was hard going in the dark and Jim was forced to find handholds to help himself. Sometimes he had to feel around for a good place to step. He couldn't afford to stumble and sprain an ankle. The going was so difficult he had to give it his full attention. He welcomed this for it gave him a respite from thinking. Then the trail leveled off.

They took a break. Jim realized he was no longer cold and he was breathing hard. He was sweating. Thirty-five degrees, almost total darkness, 8,500 feet up, and he was sweating. He took off his duster and unsnapped his vest. If he didn't dry off he'd get super chilled when they stopped. His calves and thighs were burning, knees and ankles complaining. His head was throbbing in the thin air. Buck looked over at him.

"Yeah, I know I'm kind of old for this kind of march. Am I slowing you down? You gonna carry me now?"

Buck snorted.

"Well, okay then, just give me a minute. If I get too tired I'll just grab hold of your tail and you can pull me up."

Jim knew he couldn't slack off. He had a lead by starting in the dead of night, but he was on foot. It was slower, but he needed to not exhaust Buck, at least not yet.

He loved the exertion of climbing these trails, but after this ascent he was wobbly and a bit light headed. Once he had been able to keep up a steady pace all day, but he wasn't twenty five anymore, heck, he wasn't even fifty anymore. He had no option. He had to keep going, had to get far enough ahead so he maybe could set up an ambush and spring Bob loose.

"Ambush? When did I start thinking about an ambush? Huh. What kind of ambush? My 38 is useless except at close range. Just fire off some shots? Bad idea. Maybe do something to panic the horses."

In many places, the trail was gloomy even at high noon because of the trees but every so often there was a small glade where the vegetation opened up or a tree had fallen. Where the canopy opened up the light from the moon and stars made the trek easier. The trail was very rocky – a man or a horse had to pick his footing carefully, which made the trek slow and noisy. And there were springs, several of them, which fed tiny streams which crossed the trail. He let Buck drink whenever he wanted. Even in daylight, detours from the trail would be difficult. The trail was literally on the side of the mountain and the slope was steep on either side and the underbrush was thick.

In one section, the trail snaked through a boulder field. There it was just barely wide enough for a horse or pack mule. The Forest Service had put crushed rock down between boulders to fill in places where a hoof could get stuck. The boulder field was a hundred yards or more wide and would have been impassable for the animals otherwise. Because this was within the wilderness boundary, this all had to be done by hand. Men and mules had carried the crushed rock up here and laid it down. Jim always shook his head when he thought about the effort in man hours and mule miles this must have taken.

The view to the east from the boulder field was a delight on the other occasions Jim had taken this trail. One could look down on the wooded foothills below and even see the plains off in the distance. Now, however, Jim could not marvel at the view. It was still too dark. A glance to the east revealed only the starry sky over black lumps.

He stopped. The view to the east. Shit. He should try calling the sheriff.

He'd always hated cell phones, said they were of the devil. Hated them because he couldn't get away from them. And now this cell phone was his only connection, his lifeline.

When he was a kid phones were more personal, human. The phone was on the wall, you'd pick up the ear piece and crank the handle on the wall. The local operator would answer, would know who he was, and he'd tell her the number he wanted, something like 13W.

Sometimes he'd hang out with this kid, Sid Timmerman. Sid's mom was the operator in town. When Jim's parents were working late he and Sid would go to the Village Pantry for dinner (usually hamburgers). Sid was a latch key kid long before the term was coined. Sid lived with his mother in a small apartment over the Lake Hotel. Sid never mentioned a father and Jim never thought to ask why, even though Sid was the only kid in town who didn't have a father. Not only was a one parent home a rarity fifty years ago, there seemed to be an unwritten rule that the subject was taboo.

Small towns were like that. Everybody knew everyone else's business, but some topics were never discussed around children. The adults believed that this somehow protected the kids from being infected with the ills of the world like divorce, alcoholism, homosexuality, and communism.

Jim checked the battery indicator. The charge was about half gone. Nothing he could do about that. There were two bars for service. Better call right here.

Chapter 31

Zeke had sat down on the sofa in his office. He was just going to rest his eyes for a few minutes. The cell phone in his pocket woke him. He fumbled it out and answered just before it switched to voice mail.

"Thomasen," he croaked.

"Sheriff, Jim Taylor."

"Jim," Zeke sat up and gave his head a shake, trying to clear the fog. "Where are you? What's going on?"

"Exactly what I want to know. Where are you? Are you on your way up here?"

Fully awake now, Zeke looked at his watch. "Jim, it's four thirty. I've got two deputies ready to go at first light, but I don't know where to go."

"I'm on my way up the trail to Ant Hill. Know where that is?"

Zeke got up and walked over to the map. "Yep, I see it. Where are the kidnappers?"

"They're still camped at Soldier Park. I've been going for a couple hours, trying to get way ahead of them."

"What's happened?"

"They had to turn back from the pass like I told you. I

guessed that Bob would offer them this trail, take them up past Ant Hill. Figured they'd want a way out of the mountains besides going back to Archer Mesa."

"Okay, I'll head up from Archer. I've got the FBI coming. I'll have them set up to watch Piney Creek trailhead."

"That's fine, but I'm worried about Bob. They're going to kill him sooner or later. Stevens they need, but once they get where they want Bob is surplus."

"Damn. You're probably right, but I can't do anything about it."

"I'm here and I'm going to try to free him." Jim paused, thought about what he'd just said.

"Whoa, Jim. There's what, six of them? You'll just get killed."

"Look, Sheriff…"

"Call me Zeke."

"Zeke, I'm Bob's only chance."

"Jim, just wait a minute. Let me think."

"Zeke, my phone is going to run out of juice soon. I'll call you later."

"Jim," the phone was dead.

Zeke paced around his office. I should be up there. Jim is going to get himself killed and I'm down here totally useless. Damn it, damn it, damn it.

Chapter 32

When they got to the second switchback, Jim took another break. Although it was still cold and he'd taken layers of clothes off, his shirt was soaked with sweat from the exertion. He took it off and let his body cool for a minute, then put on the spare shirt. He checked his watch – almost five o'clock. The sky would lighten soon. Time to come up with a plan.

Jim gobbled a couple of candy bars and set off again. The next switchback had no trees around it, then there was fifty yards of steep, rocky slope before the next turn. The footing was treacherous, the trail weaving between boulders, in places barely wide enough for a horse's hoof. After that turn, the trail went back into the trees. A man could hide in those trees and look straight down on the exposed switchback and straightaway. That spot would work for an ambush but he would have to get the horse much higher up to keep Buck safe and out of sight.

It took another hour of climbing the trail before they came to a spot that that satisfied Jim. They came upon a level stretch of trail going through a patch of tall pines. It was pretty much directly over the ambush site but almost a thousand feet higher and was near the crest of the trail. This would have to do. He led Buck off the trail and tied him to a tree next to a patch of grass. He made the knot loose enough so that Buck could free himself with some effort, just in case he didn't survive the ambush. He didn't want Buck stranded.

It was now full light. The others should have started out by now. He stuffed snack bars and candy in his pockets and left his heavy clothes with the horse. He hooked the hatchet on his belt and started back down the mountain.

Chapter 33

Zeke was wide awake after talking with Jim. He paced the floor, anxious to do something. Finally he went down the hall to the dispatch room. Had Nan Rodriguez call Sally at home and ask her to come in.

Sally bounded into his office twenty minutes later. Today she sported a yellow Donald Duck t-shirt, shorts, and running shoes. The shoes looked huge on her sticklike legs.

"Hi, Sheriff. You caught me as I was leaving for my morning run. What can I do?"

Zeke smiled at her enthusiasm. "Davey brought back the make and serial numbers on the ATVs the kidnappers used. Will you see if you can run down where they got them?"

"I'll do my best, but it's Sunday. I may have to leave e-mail messages and get answers tomorrow."

"See if you can at least check stolen property reports today."

"Okay."

Chapter 34

On the way down to the ambush site, he chopped down several trees so that they fell across the trail. He hoped this would slow down any pursuit. When he got closer, he ignored the trail and went straight down slope through the trees. The going was very steep and he needed both hands to grab trees and shrubs to keep his balance. It was going to be a bugger climbing back up.

Finally he got to the spot he wanted. It was directly over the exposed switchback and straight stretch. He could hide in the trees and wait. Before he hunkered down, he gathered rocks to throw. He piled up about twenty baseball sized rocks, more than he would probably have a chance to throw, but he figured he'd rather have too many than too few. Then there was nothing else to do but wait and watch. He checked his watch – 8:10.

He made himself a comfortable place to sit where he'd be concealed under pine boughs. It felt good to sit. He nibbled on a granola bar. He felt like he'd already put in a full day, could feel the long hike up the side of the mountain in his legs and the altitude in his lungs.

Jim tried not to think about what he was going to do, didn't want to psych himself out. He snorted and shook his head. Everyone back in Wisconsin would think him stark raving mad if they knew what he planned to do. He had no business mixing it up with these fuckers; he should be down below letting the authorities deal with this. They'd call him an idiot to risk his life and a damn old fool to think he could pull this off.

But that old life was over. It had been killing him slowly, grinding him up into dust. Pretty much everything was a bummer. His wife had just left him. She hadn't warned him, but the marriage had been disintegrating for quite some time and there was nothing left but a shell. A third failed marriage. His law practice, though busy, provided just enough income to keep his creditors at bay. Sixty fricking years old and he was about one paycheck away from bankruptcy. He liked to think he was good at what he did, but Julia Schultz had recently committed suicide and he should have seen it coming and prevented it. Failures, debts, and guilt. Being a grown up sucked.

When he was a kid, grade school age, he used to cry watching Peter Pan on television. (The Mary Martin version.) He cried because he didn't want to grow up, grow old, be an adult. He had never found Never Never Land and now he was over sixty. Sixty! So he had come here to the mountains to be Peter Pan and not be a grown up any more.

Before he left for Wyoming he'd been wallowing in self pity. It embarrassed him to remember that. Therapists would have said that he was 'in a bad place'. No shit. He needed to escape. So he left in hopes that living the simple life in the mountains would let that tangled mess fade into history and the present would fill him with its immediacy. Jim laughed out loud and shook his head. He'd sure gotten much more than he'd bargained for.

Yet he had never felt so alive as he had the past two days. He was truly living in the moment, conscious of the movement of his muscles with every step, his senses heightened, every sound and smell amplified. Thinking, planning, anticipating, ready to react, just like in a trial. There was no room for mistakes, consequences were dire. As a friend from college used to say, he was right here, right now.

Right now he was waiting in ambush and he needed to think about something else. He thought back to what had triggered his flight to the mountains.

He had toiled for months on a difficult malpractice case. The trial had taken two weeks. Against all odds he had won a favorable verdict. The client had killed herself within days.

Julia Schultz had hired him. Her daughter had died in a hospital. Some kind of medication screw up. She was five years old. Only child, single mother. The hospital had tried to cover it up. Julia had buried her grief in her effort to get vindication, built her life around the lawsuit.

The hospital had hired the nastiest, black-hearted lawyers, absolute assholes who took great pleasure in screwing over anyone who stood in their way, widows and orphans included. The defense had been scorched earth, denied everything, destroyed evidence, stonewalled at every turn, used every delaying tactic in the book. They'd even attacked this grieving mother, insinuating that she was only in it for the money.

Julia attended every deposition and hearing and bombarded Jim with calls, letters, e-mails, and articles. Wrote out lists of questions for him to ask. Demanded explanations for every tactic he employed. She had driven Jim batty. He pushed her away, ignored her as much as he could.

The trail below was lit by the sun. He had an almost vertical perspective. There was no sign or sound of the kidnappers. The spot below was as near perfect for this ambush as could be. It was a good plan. It would work. It had to.

The judge sent the jury out to deliberate.

Jim had given one of his finest closing arguments. As soon as the jury left the courtroom, he started packing his files and notes into his big, battered brief case. The courtroom emptied out. Soon he and Julia were the only people left. He looked around. The judge's bench, the witness box, the court reporter's chair all neat and tidy. A person looking in would have no idea that this had been the scene of battle, an emotional roller coaster of a trial.

He had put his heart and soul into the effort and now he was spent, exhausted. The jury was out. There was nothing more he could do. The trial, the strategy and preparation, the presentation, the anticipation and the counter moves, had consumed his every waking minute for the entire two weeks. Whether eating, dressing, even brushing his teeth, all he thought about was the trial. He'd even slept with a pen and paper next to his bed in case he thought of something in the middle of the night. Now he just wanted to leave, be somewhere else, think about anything but the case.

Sitting exhausted at counsel table, Julia Schultz looked over at him.

"You're going to wait here with me, aren't you?"

"No, Julia, I'm going back to the office and put my feet up. I'll wait for them to call me with the verdict."

"You won't even come here for the verdict?" A quiver in her voice that he chose to ignore.

"Nope. I've done all I can. No point coming back here, I'll get it over the phone."

Stony faced, she turned away.

What an asshole he was. And that was the last time he'd see her.

He'd tried so many jury cases that he no longer bothered to sit in the courthouse to wait for the verdict. Tired, jaded, uncaring. Whatever.

He'd get to know his clients too well, know all their faults and warts and foibles. To do a proper job he had to feel as much of their pain and anguish as was possible, but to protect himself (that was the excuse, anyway) he had to turn it off when he wasn't working on the case.

So much of his sense of self worth came from knowing that he always did his best for his clients. When he took on a client's case it meant a commitment that was not limited to the courtroom or preparation for trial. Cases were clients and clients were real people, people with all kinds of needs and problems, physical, financial, psychological, emotional. Clients often became tremendously dependent on their lawyer, looking to him for advice and solutions. He counseled them, served as therapist and priest at times, made sure they got to

123

the right specialists, be it for surgery, bankruptcy, or divorce. He had failed Julia. He had failed himself.

Looking back now, he could see that he'd become an insensitive bastard.

He should have realized that when the case was over she would have no reason to go on living. He had known other clients who had become severely depressed when their cases had concluded. Take away the object of obsession and the person could become lost, rootless. He should have been more supportive and should have insisted that she seek therapy during the litigation. He hadn't given this a thought. He had been callous and selfish. He had just treated her obsession as an irritation, something to be avoided. And then she was dead.

As a lawyer he'd always wanted to do his best and over the years he'd become very, very good. He put a tremendous amount of mental and emotional effort into winning. But at some point winning had become more important than helping the client. Clients had become a means to an end.

Where were they? They had to be coming up this trail. Had to be. If they weren't coming, he'd fucked up big time. He hadn't waited to see if they'd started up this way. Shit. Had he misled the sheriff? The kidnappers could have gone back to the camp after all or headed for Archer. Either one could be a disaster if the sheriff was on his way up.

His only outlet in the past months had been Buck. Grooming him and riding him had been therapy. When he was riding Buck he didn't think about anything else, just lived in the moment, focused on the horse. Thirty five years ago he had learned how to fly a light plane. He had given that the same total concentration. The trouble with flying was that it couldn't be done at the spur of the moment. You'd have to reserve a plane, check the weather, prepare and file a flight plan, and then get permission from the tower to take off. Besides, an airplane didn't talk to him or react to what he said or nuzzle him. It was just a machine, had no life or thought of its own. Living on the farm, the horse was always available and in ten minutes could be groomed, saddled, and ready. If the weather was bad they could trailer over to a neighbor who had an indoor riding arena.

Yes, Buck had kept him sane. So had living on the farm and taking care of the horses. It got him out in the barn early in the morning. Feeding the horses was a great way to start the day. They were always happy to see him and they would talk to him. Each horse had a different voice. They would start calling to him as soon as they heard the door to the house open and close. By the time he walked into the barn, every horse was bright eyed and cheerful.

Each horse had its own routine when he entered the barn. Lacy, the lead mare, would pee as soon as Jim entered. Eddie would start banging his feed bucket with his nose. Portia paced in her stall. Buck would hang his head out of his stall, focus his bright eyes on Jim, and nicker. When he left the barn to feed the two mares who lived outside, those two would have their eyes and ears focused on the barn door. Jim would whistle a few bars of "Dixie" to Dixie and Dolly to assure them that food was indeed was on its way. The horses' needs were simple. He loved them and they returned his love unconditionally.

They had to be coming. It was the only choice that made any sense. The high water in the creek would keep them from camp. Going to Archer trailhead would be stupid. They had to know that cops would be there. "Just settle down, Jim. They're coming. Settle down and wait. Remember Zeno's paradox."

He considered himself an expert at waiting. Waiting for judges, waiting for doctors. He used to joke that if he had a nickel for every minute he spent waiting, he would be able to retire. He had all kinds of tricks to help pass the time such as trying to remember the details of books he had recently read or the exact lyrics of a favorite song.

Here in the wilderness, waiting was easy for he never tired of watching the trees and sky and listening to the sounds around him – the wind, small animal noises, insects, birds. Nature was always entertaining for him. And he savored the absence of city noises and smells. He hated city noises – traffic, sirens, construction, loud music from cars and boom boxes, people talking on cell phones – an assault on his ears and his peace of mind. If he was lucky, these sounds became white noise that could be tuned out. Up in the mountains he didn't need or want to tune his surroundings out.

He could usually find peace on his farm in Wisconsin. His favorite time for noise on the farm was summer nights. He would sit on the porch with a cold Bass Ale and be soothed by the orchestral chirping of crickets. Some nights he would hear the coyotes singing in the distance. Singing was an apt word for it. The high pitched yipping and wailing did have a musical quality. He also loved the sounds the horses made at night, snuffling, grunting, scraping teeth on stable walls, munching on hay, the occasional banging on a feed bucket. Horses had an amazing variety of noises.

Jim started as heard the clatter of horse shoes on rock, then voices. He pulled out the binoculars and focused on the switchback.

Chapter 35

Bob had always enjoyed the ride up to Ant Hill. Even though he'd done it more times than he could remember, he never tired of the scenery. The trail was cut into the side of the mountain, most of it through dense forest. There were tiny springs and rivulets surrounded with lush grass and boulders covered with lichen. Best of all were the places where the trees gave way and revealed views to the east. Foothills dark green with pine undulated downward toward tan open country. It gave him a sense of how high up he was.

Today, as usual, he was leading a string of mules. It was an easy task here because the trail was narrow and there were no detours that a mule could stray onto. He was in the middle of the caravan, the bald guy, Jack, in the way back and the scrawny, shifty one, Botts, leading. The rest of the men were spread out along the line. Chet was near the front. No one seemed to be paying him much attention. Huh.

Bob could feel eyes boring into his back, knew it was Jack. He'd seen him shoot Dave. The guy had shown no emotion when he'd done it. The man exuded a sense of violence, not the reckless violence of a barroom fighter, but a controlled violence, a ruthlessness to be used when needed. Jack scared him and he knew that the bastard wouldn't hesitate to kill him when he was no longer needed.

He had to get away to save himself. If he tried to escape and failed, he'd be shot. Bob figured the horses were the key. None of these men were horsemen. They were perched awkwardly on the saddles, shifting around, yanking on the reins, making the horses goosey. They weren't really in control of the horses, the animals just followed the one in front out of habit. Most of the men were moaning and groaning and lifting their butts out of the saddle. Bob smiled to himself. They were blistered and raw.

Where was Jim? He figured he was out there somewhere, thinking and planning, like those signs he'd left along the trail. A clear message that he knew they'd have to turn back from the pass. Jim had been up here often enough over the years to know his way around. Jim had been moody this summer, avoided going to town, content to keep to himself. Bob trusted him, knew him to be a stand up guy. He'd come out this year and wanted to help for the summer, didn't even ask for pay. Bob could tell he was running away, but Jim said nothing about what was eating at him. Would Jim try something or was he just spying for the sheriff? Best to be ready for any chance that came along. There'd be no second chance.

Chapter 36

He waited under the pine boughs, deep in shade. He felt a breeze brush his face. He shifted, making sure his butt and legs hadn't gone numb. The approaching riders were still under the green canopy and shaded from light by the thick growth on both sides of the trail. They were just noise to his senses, but his reptile brain knew better. He shivered. Down there was death, nasty, unforgiving death. That primitive part of his brain was telling him to run away.

Everything around the switchback was sharp and clearly contrasted in the morning sun. Beyond the switchback he could see the lower hills, dark green flowing with the contours, almost black in the valleys. At the switchback the rocks hemming in the trail looked huge from his angle and the slope of the trail seemed too steep. Would they dismount and lead the horses? There were six of them and one of him. What would he do if they were on foot? He could still back out of this, sneak up the trail and run away. No, running away was not an option. If they were on foot he'd back off and wait for another opportunity.

The clatter got closer, the voices clearer. Someone was griping about blisters on his ass. Jim saw movement in the trees near the switchback.

He'd just send some rocks down at the exposed party and create enough of a distraction to allow Bob to jump off his horse and escape into the woods downhill. If Bob stayed off the trail, it would be almost impossible to catch him. Jim would then climb back up to Buck and get off the mountain as fast as he could. Just throw rocks at six armed men and get away without getting shot.

"Sounds easy, Jim. Keep telling yourself that and maybe you'll believe it."

Yeah, but he had never been very accurate at throwing a baseball. A decent catcher, but a wild pitcher, as likely to hit the batter as the strike zone. Huh, maybe that would pay off here. Or maybe not. Maybe this was a really stupid plan and all he'd accomplish would be his own death. This was madness.

The lead rider came into view. Long dark hair, looking down at the rocks. Good, he had his rifle slung on his shoulder. It would be useless for at least a minute even if the guy could aim on horseback. Jim grabbed a rock, wanted to throw it now, just do this thing. He was cranked up tight, ready to let fly. With an effort he held himself back, made himself wait until everyone was exposed. Had to see where Bob was.

The others came up to the switchback. They all had their guns slung. They looked tired, heads down, shoulders slumped. Bob and the mules were in the middle, three men in front, three behind. Bob had his head up, alert, looking around. Chet was second in line, looked asleep. The horses were slipping on the rocks, their riders stupidly steering them, not letting them pick their own way. The following horses were bunching up, bumping into one another, ears pinned back, teeth showing, and tails twitching. A tremendous clatter of horse shoes on the rocks. It was a train wreck waiting to happen.

The scene below was perfect. Jim took a deep breath. He forced all the tension from his body. He felt like he was about to jump off a cliff. "Focus, you can do this." He exhaled. Got that 'what the fuck, just do it' feeling he got when he'd stand up to address the jury, all doubts forgotten. "Now."

Okay. First a rock at the guys in back of Bob. Jim stood up and hurled the rock down at the next to last rider. It was heavier than a baseball and bounced off a boulder only half way there. His heart sank, a miss. But the bounce was lucky. In what seemed like slow motion, the rock sailed right at the man. It hit him square in the chest and he went flying off the horse backwards.

"Geez, don't just stand there watching." Jim grabbed another rock and hurled it at the lead riders. It missed, not even close, but the rock started a small cascade of rocks that rolled down onto the trail and around the hooves of the nervous animals. All the horses and mules started jumping and prancing, confined on the rocky slope, panicked with nowhere to flee, their eyes wild and nostrils flared. The killers were flopping around in their saddles, barely able to hang on.

He saw Bob leap off his horse and, dodging the jumbled, panicked animals, run down into the trees. "Yes, it's working. Keep it up. Give Bob some time." He squatted down and got hold of a rock the size of a basketball. He half shoved, half threw it at the middle of the jumble of horses and riders. The rock rolled then bounced and flew over the tangle of men and animals. It smacked into a boulder on the other side of the trail with a huge bang and sent rock splinters flying.

The animals started to squeal and bellow, frantic to escape, spinning around, heads and tails high.

All the men were shouting now which only made the horses more skittish. Jim quickly tossed two more rocks. One hit the third mule. No longer held by Bob, the mule gave a huge bray and started bucking and kicking on the narrow, steep switchback, totally out of control of itself. It crashed into the horse behind it. With an angry bray, the mule fired a double barreled kick, standing on its front legs, both rear legs shooting backwards. That horse had nowhere to go, hemmed in by rocks and the other panicked animals behind and the crazed mule in front. The horse lost its footing and with a scream fell on its side, crushing the rider between it and the rocks.

For a few seconds he stood in the open just staring in awe at the chaos and mayhem he'd caused.

One of the remaining riders had spotted Jim. He shouted and pointed.

Time to go. Jim turned and started climbing straight up into the trees, hands grabbing trees and shrubs, feet scrabbling in the dirt and rocks like a woodchuck chased by a hound.

Within a minute or so he heard gunshots, lots of them. Bullets were ricocheting off rocks. The whine of the bullets and the brang of the ricochets made him cringe. He felt naked, totally exposed. He could not afford to stop and take cover. He had to keep moving. Jim kept telling himself that they were shooting blind.

Chapter 37

Bob saw the rock hit and bounce, heard the cry from behind, knew a man had been hit. He looked in the direction from where the rock had come. Even before he saw Jim throw again, he knew this was it.

He watched the growing panic in front turn to chaos. Then he looked over his shoulder. A man was down and everyone else was just trying to stay on his mount, the horses bouncing and turning, the men flopping. It was now or never.

For a second he thought about Chet Stevens. Chet was hanging onto the saddle horn for dear life. There was no way he could get his attention and couldn't get near him. They wouldn't harm Chet; he was their prize.

Bob dropped the lead rope for the mules, swung his right leg over the front of the saddle while pulling his left foot out of the stirrup, and launched himself off the horse. He landed on all fours and scrambled away from the trail. Within seconds he was on his feet and running down slope through the maze of trees. The slope gave him momentum as he leaped over rocks and logs, hurtling down the mountain.

He could hear the shouts of the men and the squeals and bellows and brays of the animals. After a minute he slowed his headlong plunge and got behind a thick clump of pines. The last thing he needed was a broken leg. Bob tried to catch his breath and listened for pursuit.

Over the noise of the animals he heard someone yelling, "Larry's down, help him!" Another voice, Jack's, shouting "Where's the guide?" And Botts, "Up there. There's a guy up there!"

He heard Jack again, "To hell with Larry. Shoot that bastard up there!" Then gunfire and more clatter of horse shoes on rocks. He thought for a moment about Jim, prayed he wouldn't get hit, figured the men couldn't really aim while their horses were bouncing and turning.

Bob heard a crashing and pounding coming at him and saw two riderless horses blundering through the trees, one coming right at him. Head high, eyes wide, whites showing, nostrils flared, the horse was in full panicked flight. It went past within a few feet of his hiding place.

He turned and followed the horse. Maybe he could catch it. He'd get farther away anyhow. He breathed a silent "thank you" to Jim.

Chapter 38

Jim scrambled hand over foot. He crossed the trail and kept going, frantic with bullets still whining and snapping wildly hitting trees and rocks. The slope was brutal, he guessed over forty five degrees, and he had to grab trees and shrubs to pull himself up.

When he hit the trail a second time he had to stop. The climb had been a blur. He had climbed like a machine, constantly going onward, without pause, without any thought other than getting away from the shooters. He collapsed to his knees on the trail.

Jim was gasping for breath in the thin air. His lungs were on fire and he was lightheaded, his pulse throbbing in his ears. It felt like a steel band was tightening around his head. His vision darkened and he thought he was going to faint.

Jim fell forward onto his hands and tried to control his breathing. As he finally caught enough oxygen his vision cleared. And then he felt the fire in the muscles of his arms and legs. He realized he was drenched in sweat. He stripped down to his t-shirt. He replayed what had happened: Bob had escaped and he had probably injured two of the killers. He had pulled it off. He had done it. Now it was time to leave.

There was no time for self congratulation. There was a gang of very angry men coming up after him. If they caught up, they would surely kill him. He had to keep moving, get his horse, and get off the mountain to safety. He did not want to see those men ever again.

He set off on the trail now as the going was easier that way. He figured that the killers would stay on the horses and lead the mules. They had to know that their only hope was to keep on the trail. The horses would go faster than Jim on foot but the road blocks he had set up would slow them down, forcing detours into thick brush.

He hiked steadily up the trail pacing himself so he wouldn't need to take rest breaks, had to force himself not to hurry. He could feel them behind him; they were coming for him. He'd gone about twenty minutes when he heard noise up the trail.

Jim stopped and listened. Hoofbeats. What was this?

Could they have gotten around him somehow? Did they have more men coming from the Piney Creek trailhead? Jesus! Was he trapped between the men chasing him and more of them coming down the trail?

Chapter 39

Bob caught up with the horse when its reins got tangled in brush. It was sweating, its breathing labored, blowing. The horse's eyes were wild and it was quivering. He approached from the side slowly and talked soothingly. He got within a few feet of its head and just stood, hands at his side.

"Easy, Ralph. Things are okay now."

Away upslope the wild shooting stopped. Bob reckoned that shots from bouncing horses had almost no chance of hitting Jim. Jim should escape unharmed and make his way to the trailhead.

As silence returned to the woods the horse calmed, its breathing slowed and the wild look faded from its eye. When it gave a great sigh and lowered its head Bob took two slow steps and stroked its neck.

Five minutes later he'd untangled the reins and was leading Ralph back up the slope, wending his way around boulders and trees. When they finally got back to the trail Bob stopped and listened. The last thing he wanted was to stumble into the kidnappers.

Chapter 40

Jim took cover in the thick brush off the trail. The hoof beats were getting closer. A clatter of a horseshoe on a rock. He crouched lower and thought about what to do. He could shoot, but he didn't know where the others were. A shot would bring them. He guessed his best option was to lay low and then climb higher and hole up. But what about Buck? Had they found him? Could he sneak up to where he'd left Buck?

The hoof beats stopped.

A horse snorted.

The hoof beats started again.

There was the crunch and scratch of brush, the rider was going off the trail right toward him. Shit.

Jim crouched even lower. He pulled his gun and pointed it straight ahead and up.

Then there was silence. Jim held his breath. Back off. Go away, please.

A horse's muzzle poked through the brush right in front of his face and breathed on him.

Buck!

Jim rode Buck up to where he had tied him. He dumped

the panniers and backpacks. He took one pack and loaded it with some horse feed, snack bars, rope, hatchet and the scotch. Everything else he threw in the panniers and covered them with brush. He hung the pack on the saddle horn and swung up in the saddle. "Buck, we're out of here."

Chapter 41

All was quiet. The kidnappers must have moved on. Bob was just about ready to mount up and head down away from this mountain and back to town. There was nothing he could do up here. He'd find the sheriff and tell him where these bastards were heading. Then he heard the booming echo of a rifle shot.

Damn. They'd left a sniper and that shot was surely aimed at Jim. Jim must have been at the top of the trail where the trees and brush gave way and there was a clear shot from below.

Did he get Jim? It was a really long shot to take uphill. A couple of these guys seemed to be ex-military. The shot was possible. Bob shook his head, hands clenched in fists. If he'd had a gun he'd go get that sniper.

After a few minutes he heard the clatter of horseshoes on rock. The sniper had mounted up and was following the rest of his crew. Bob waited ten minutes then followed. He had to find out what had happened to Jim.

Chapter 42

It was a relief to ride. Within thirty minutes they were at the crest of the trail. The top of Ant Hill was another fifteen hundred feet up and to the south, a massive pile of gray boulders and scree. It did look like an ant hill, although to Jim's eye it was a pyramid. The trail went along a ridge at the top of the slope for about a half a mile and then went up and over the ridge to a gentle grassy slope another mile before passing under trees again. They would be exposed until then but Jim figured he had a pretty good lead on the killers.

At the top of the trail, the ground leveled off. The lay of the land was more or less a plateau with Ant Hill Mountain forming the southern border and Cloud Peak the western. To the east was a steep drop to the foothills and then the plains. Trees, miles and miles of trees, stretched to the north.

The trail cut diagonally across the plateau, passing shallow lakes and small streams. Jim aimed to get to Cloud Peak reservoir on the west. In the past he'd caught lots of trout in its deep, cold water. Below the reservoir were Piney Creek and its two lakes, Flat Iron and Frying Pan. Beyond the reservoir towered a line of dark, granite peaks including

Cloud Peak at over 13,000 feet. The plateau itself was about 10,000 feet in elevation. It had been a wonderful, isolated place to camp and fish but now these bastards would foul it. Today he would pass through and connect with a rough road that led down to Piney Creek trailhead.

They were moseying along the edge of the plateau, cooling down after the final, steep climb, Jim thinking about the route they would take to leave these killers behind. Crack! Something hit a boulder about three feet away. Jim felt rock splinters pepper his clothes. Then came the boom of a rifle shot.

As Buck took off in a gallop, Jim looked down the mountain. One of the kidnappers had walked out onto a boulder field. He could see the glint of the scope. They raced until they were screened by an elephant sized boulder. Jim realized he had been holding his breath. His stomach was knotted up, his hands shaking. "Jesus, Buck, that was close." Buck was breathing hard, ears twitching, looking all around. After Buck's breathing slowed, they set off at a walk heading west.

If they could get under the trees, their pursuers would not have another clear shot at them. Unless they caught up, and that was unlikely, bringing the mules would slow them down, especially without Bob to handle them. Jim guessed that the others were riding while their buddy played sniper. They would be at least a half hour behind him if they didn't wait for the sniper to join them.

Jim asked Buck for a jog trot. "When we get under the trees, we'll take a good rest. We can watch the crest from the edge of the woods."

Twenty minutes later they were in the trees. Jim steered Buck off the trail and into a thick stand of lodge pole pines. It was dark enough under the pines to make them invisible to a distant observer. Jim got down and let Buck graze while he held the reins. He got out the binoculars and watched the crest.

Half an hour went by and he started to relax, the adrenalin wearing off. He wanted a cup of coffee and some hot food. His stomach grumbled at the thought. He and Buck were alive and unhurt. They were going to escape this mess. He just wanted to make sure that they hadn't recaptured Bob, then he and Buck would get out.

Even though he was expecting them, he was startled when he saw the kidnappers at the crest. He wanted to throw up, but he swallowed, clenched his teeth, and watched them assemble after their climb.

There were five men on horseback. He could see Chet in the middle of the troop. One was slumped in the saddle, had to be a victim of the rock attack. The group stopped. One of them had binoculars, probably Bob's, and was looking north toward where Jim and Buck were hiding. They did not have Bob with them.

"Man oh man, Buck. I'm thinking of that song, If I Had A Rocket Launcher. I'm such a poor shot that's the only way I could hit them, but that would get those miserable horses, too. I don't have a ghost of a chance of hitting anyone with my 38, it would just give away our position. They're going to wait for their sniper buddy so I think we'd be better off just going. I hope we never see those bastards again."

They could leave this mess behind now, would never see the kidnappers again. Jim blew out a breath and mounted up. They kept in the trees until the first bend in the trail screened them from view. They still had a long ride ahead, but Jim figured they'd be down from the mountains by nightfall.

Chapter 43

"What do you mean I can't go up there?" Eyes blazing, Zeke was in the agent's face. He looked about ready to bite the guy's head off and use it for a spittoon.

"Sir, the Special Agent In Charge has instructed me to assume jurisdiction. It is a national forest, federal land. We're closing all access points near the subjects. My orders are to allow the ransom to be delivered as demanded. We will watch that trailhead from a distance and be ready to move in once the hostage is freed."

"So you've talked with the family?"

"Yes, Sheriff, and were told the detailed directions given by the kidnappers. We can't allow them to see any law enforcement in their area."

"What about the other man they've taken? He'll probably be killed with or without the ransom."

"Sorry, but I've got my orders. We don't know that he'll be killed."

Zeke stomped out of the building and stood outside, his face bright red and his fists clenched. He spat in the dust. No point in taking it out on the agent. He was following orders.

He looked up at the mountains. He mumbled an apology to Bob and Jim. They were totally on their own. No help would be coming. God damn politicians were running the show. He spat again.

To hell with the FBI and the damn politicians. He'd send Davey Hopkins up there. Not all the way, but close enough to make sure the kidnappers didn't backtrack from Ant Hill and try for the pass again.

Chapter 44

They were finally at the top of the trail. Big Jack called a halt and took out the map he had taken from the guide. He could see they were on the plateau and that the reservoir was west of where they were. He gathered the men around.

The three youngsters were quiet, hanging their heads, looking scared.

"Listen up you sorry bastards. One of your buddies got killed. That's part of the job, so get over it. The fucker who killed Larry is out there somewhere. If he shows his face, we're gonna to kill him." He paused, looked each one in the eye. "Stay alert. We'll be at the reservoir soon and you can get off these damn horses. We wait until Botts gets here."

He would not let this mission go sideways. A freaking ambush! Who was that guy? Maybe it was that fucking assistant. He'd asked Chet, but Chet had been so busy trying to stay on his horse that he hadn't even seen the son-of-a-bitch.

The guide was gone, one man killed, and these stupid kids were spooked. Shit. The guy was probably long gone now that the guide was free. Thank god he had Botts. Botts was as tough as they come, been in some real tight spots, never panicked. Botts and Horvath had covered for him when he'd shot that Iraqi kid. Yeah, they had his back.

Chapter 45

Zeke was still standing in the parking lot when a Forest Service pick-up zoomed into the lot, braked abruptly, and a ranger jumped out. The ranger jogged up to him. When he got a good look at Zeke's face he hesitated.

Zeke spoke first. "Howdy, Tim. What's the hurry?"

"I heard about the situation up there. I know you've got your hands full but I just got a call from the north district office."

"Spit it out, Tim."

"They heard about the kidnapping and the shooting. They called to warn us that a troop of boy scouts had hiked in from their district and planned to hike out down here. They're due to come out in a couple of days. Nobody knows exactly where they might be now."

"Oh, God." Zeke shook his head and looked up at the sky. "You better come inside and tell the FBI."

Zeke, the ranger, and the FBI agent studied the map on the wall of Zeke's office.

The ranger pointed. "They hiked in here, said they would go south. They brought along food but planned to catch fish to supplement what they packed. Supposed to be a two week trip so they couldn't carry all their food. According to the plan they left with the northern district office they were to come out a day or two from now."

"They say which trailhead they would come out?" Zeke asked.

"Didn't say which trailhead. Supposed to be coming out near our town."

"That narrows it down to either Archer or Piney Creek." Zeke circled the two points on the map. "And the kidnappers are supposed to be at the reservoir here." He circled again. "Which is right between the two trailheads."

The ranger cleared his throat. "With twenty kids to feed you can't count on fishing one of the creeks. So that makes the reservoir a likely spot for them."

The two looked over at the FBI agent.

"There's a good chance those scouts are right up there in the middle of this."

Agent Janns nodded. "Okay, Sheriff. I'll call my boss."

Zeke and the ranger had coffee while they waited for the agent to make his call.

"Zeke, what are you going to do?"

"Tim, I don't know. I'm going crazy sitting down here. The FBI has taken this over. I've got to wait on them."

Agent Janns came back ten minutes later. Zeke stood. "Well, what's the plan?"

The agent stared at the map, wouldn't look at Zeke. "My orders are to hold tight. We don't know for sure that the scouts are up there."

"What?" Zeke growled.

"I don't like it either, Sheriff, but those are my orders." He looked over his shoulder and closed the door. "My boss doesn't like it either. He got a call from the deputy director in Washington. Somebody's pulled some strings."

"Shit, that's why I've got no help from Cheyenne. I thought you guys were above all that."

The agent sat down and looked at the floor. "I did too, Sheriff. I did too."

The ranger shook his head. "So nobody can do anything?"

Neither the sheriff nor the agent answered.

Chapter 46

When he got to the top of the trail Bob stopped and listened. Hearing nothing, he rode ahead a hundred yards to a stand of pines. He tied the horse to a tree and walked over to a big, dead tree that stood clear of the others.

The tree had been dead for years, weathered to where its bark had fallen off and its branches bare. Bob jumped up and grabbed the first branch. Then he climbed up using the bare stumps of the limbs as steps on a ladder.

Ten feet up gave him a clear view of the ridge and the start of the trail to the reservoir. He knew the kidnappers would head that way so he scanned to the west. The last two riders and the mules were just passing under the trees as the trail wound into the woods. Bob surveyed all around. No sign of Jim, dead or alive, or Jim's horse. The sniper had missed.

Bob smiled with relief. Then he climbed back down and mounted his horse. He thought for a moment. "Oh, hell." He loped the horse after the kidnappers.

Chapter 47

To conserve Buck's energy Jim kept them at a walk; they had a good enough lead. He'd been on this trail before. It passed near Gem Lake and then dropped down to Cloud Peak Reservoir and Piney Creek. There it connected to a rough road that was passable for ATVs. The road went down out of the mountains to a parking lot a few miles north of town. It would be full dark by the time they got to the parking lot.

The trail was well marked so the kidnappers would have no trouble following it. He didn't know whether they were going all the way down or staying somewhere. If they were going straight down to the trailhead, the sheriff needed to be told. Jim decided to hold off on calling the sheriff until he knew more because he didn't know how much charge he had left in his cell phone. If he and Buck kept moving, they would be able to get out of the way if the sheriff wanted to jump the kidnappers at the trailhead.

The trail wove through dense pine interspersed with sunny meadows, the dark green pines looking all the darker when contrasted with the pale green grass. There was no hint of the rain and snow they had endured. The air was warm and still. The only noise was Buck's footfalls on the dusty trail. They passed near Elk Lake, several acres of still water which reflected high clouds and the surrounding mountain peaks. The greens of the grass and trees gave way to the gray of boulders on one side of the lake, all seemed puny compared with the line of granite peaks in the background. They crossed a tiny stream, the turf mushy with oozing water. Red, yellow, blue wildflowers stood out in the bright sunlight. Several moose grazed nearby. They gave the moose a wide berth.

They were almost at Cloud Peak Reservoir when Buck pricked up his ears. Jim saw Buck react and looked around. The fricking flatlanders were behind them. What did Buck hear? Then Jim heard, too.

There were voices ahead. Many voices. Young voices. They came around a bend in the trail and saw the source: at least a dozen boys toting big packs.

"Ah, shit, Buck, it was too easy wasn't it?" What was he going to do? The kidnappers were coming down the trail. If they came upon these boys, the boys would be in danger for sure, maybe kept as hostages, maybe even shot. He had to get these boys out of the way and quick.

The horse grunted and dropped manure.

Jim halted. He looked at the lead boy, a teenager, wearing a Cardinals ball cap. "Son, you are walking into a peck of trouble. You and your crew have to get off the trail and well into the trees completely out of sight."

"What's the problem, sir?" asked the lead boy, as the others gathered around.

Jim explained the situation. "There's a group of armed men coming down the trail behind me. I saw them shoot a man, kill him, and they've kidnapped another. The sheriff is after them. You do not want to be in the crossfire."

"Now look, we haven't much time. Get into the woods there to the south as quickly and quietly as you can. Those men will be here in thirty minutes or so. I reckon they'll keep going but don't take any chances. Wait until full dark before you come back here. No, better yet, have a cold camp tonight and I'll send a deputy to check on you tomorrow."

The lead boy was maybe fifteen years old at the most, clean cut in appearance, dressed in a boy scout shirt and shorts. He spoke respectfully. "Sir, we can do that but there's a problem. Six of our guys are back at the reservoir fishing for our supper. Our leader's with them."

"Wonderful." Jim grimaced. "I'll see to them. You guys get going now."

Jim waited until the boys were well off the trail and then asked Buck for a trot. In less than fifteen minutes they were at the intersection of the trail and the ATV road. The dam which created the reservoir was forty yards to the west. He could see several boys fishing along the dam.

Cloud Peak and her sister mountains towered over the reservoir. Even in high summer there was snow on the tops of the mountains. Today, in the calm air, the reflection of these mountains and the clouds and the deep blue sky on the water of the reservoir was almost as spectacular as the mountains themselves. Jim had no time to enjoy the view. He had to get these boys out of sight. When the kidnappers came along they would see the boys for sure.

They went down to the overflow stream and quickly waded across it. Buck climbed up onto the dam. Jim hollered to the nearest boys. "Trouble coming down the trail. Get everybody out of sight now. There's a pack of armed killers coming this way."

Up close the boys appeared to be no more than twelve or thirteen years old. They stared at Jim and Buck, jaws slack, mouths parted, clearly confused.

"Look, boys. You've got maybe ten minutes to get yourselves and anyone else out of sight. The other guys from your group, the ones on the trail, they're already hiding. Where's your scout master or whatever he is?"

The boys pointed to the far end of the dam where a taller figure was casting out into the water. Jim asked Buck for a trot. Gravel flying, they pulled up to the leader in less than thirty seconds.

The young man looked up. He was dressed like the boys and Jim guessed he was about eighteen. Jim didn't waste time. "Howdy, I'm Jim Taylor. I'm working with Sheriff Thomasen of Flint County. You've got to get your boys back over there and into the woods. I've got the rest of your troop in there already. Kidnappers are headed this way. They've already killed someone." He paused to catch his breath. "No time to explain. You can call the sheriff to confirm this, but hide your boys first. I'll do what I can to slow them down, buy you some time, but I can't be sure so you've got to hurry."

The young man stood there, his mouth gaping, brow furrowed.

"Look, do you want to be responsible for your boys getting hurt? Move it."

Jim's courtroom voice did the trick. The leader motioned to his boys and started moving his troop toward the trees.

As Buck trotted back across the dam, Jim realized that buying more time for the scouts was easier said than done. He looked around. They'd have to get away from the reservoir, get away from the scouts. The only way to buy time was to somehow slow the kidnappers down. But how? What would slow them down?

Chapter 48

The three men were still in Zeke's office contemplating the potential disaster when there was a knock on the door.

Doris stuck her head in, glasses on the end of her nose, beads dangling.

"Sheriff, there's a call for you. Some scout leader wants to know if a Jim Taylor works for you."

The sheriff, the agent, and the ranger looked at one another, eyes wide. Agent Janns nodded to the sheriff. Zeke put the call on speaker.

"This is Sheriff Thomasen."

"Sir, I'm John Logan, leader of Troop 34, St. Loius, Missouri. We've got a problem up here."

Zeke blew out a breath. "Where are you, son?"

"Near Cloud Peak Reservoir. This guy rode up on a horse. Said he was Jim Taylor and worked for you. Told us to run and hide in the woods, there were killers coming."

Zeke glanced at the FBI agent. "That's right. You do what he tells you. If Mr. Taylor says to hurry you damn well better."

"Yes, sir."

"What else did he tell you?"

"He said he'd try to buy us some time and he'd have a deputy come for us tomorrow."

"You do exactly what he said. Get deep in the woods and don't come out 'til someone comes for you."

"Yes, sir."

"Get going now."

Zeke hung up. He closed his eyes for a moment. Man, he owed Jim Taylor. What a giant mess.

"Agent Janns, I can hear your questions. Jim Taylor is Lundsten's assistant. I asked him to be my eyes and ears. He's kept me informed as best he could."

"Can we trust him?"

"The smart alec answer is we don't have a choice. But we checked him out. He's a lawyer from Wisconsin helping his old friend Bob Lundsten. He is who he says he is. We're damn lucky to have him." And I wonder how Jim is going to buy those scouts time.

"Can you get in touch with him?"

"Only when he calls, says his cell phone is running low." Zeke eyed the closed door then faced the agent. "Look, speaking of checking people out, I have a suspicion. Something doesn't smell right. How did the kidnappers know where to find Stevens? They went right to the camp in the middle of the wilderness. They had to be tipped off." He frowned. "Another thing. The nanny told me Stevens wasn't scared, just angry. Why would that be? Can you run an asset check on Chet Stevens, Jr.? And check West Slope records. See if they've ever employed a big, bald headed guy, security maybe. You have resources I don't have."

The agent looked down then back at the sheriff, nodded. "Yeah, I get it. I'll put my people on it ASAP."

Chapter 49

As he and Buck rode away from the reservoir Jim was racking his brain trying to figure out how to slow those bastards down. He was desperate. He needed to come up with something. He closed his eyes for a moment. "What would Reacher do?" Jack Reacher was one of his favorite fictional characters, a brash but calculating hero, an irresistible force. "I'm not Reacher. He'd attack all those guys and have them dead or down in seconds."

Jim knew his options were limited. Throwing rocks would just get him shot. He had no time to set up a roadblock. The only thing he could think of was to shoot at them, lure them like a mother killdeer, get them to chase him to the north, away from the scouts. He figured that after the ambush that freed Bob they'd be looking for revenge. Maybe he wasn't Reacher but he had something that gave him an edge, something Reacher didn't have, Buck. He'd get farther away from the scouts and find a good place for an ambush.

As they trotted back on the trail, a light drizzle started. "Good, this will keep their heads down," Jim muttered. He couldn't believe he was going to tempt fate again, but reckoned he had to do it. When they got to a dogleg in the trail Jim guided Buck to the north side of the trail and into the trees. He found a spot partially screened by low trees and scrub. They had a good view for about a hundred yards up the trail.

The last thing he wanted was to see those fuckers again, but he had to buy time for the boy scouts. He sighed and shook himself. He got out the binoculars and hung them around his neck. He checked his gun and took extra bullets out of his saddle bag and put them in his duster pocket and snapped it closed, pulled his hat down and tightened the stampede strap. He was ready. He sat on the horse and waited. He tried to keep his thoughts on the scouts, not wanting to think about what he was going to do.

The gun. I'm going to use my gun. I'm going to shoot at a bunch of armed men. Ah, man. Even though he was sweating, a chill ran down his spine. He must have shook a little. Buck turned to look at him. "I'm okay, Bud. Just a little edgy. Hang with me. I'm going to need you to pull this off." They settled in to wait. It was quiet, their breathing the only sound in the stillness.

The Smith and Wesson was a simple gun, a revolver which held five rounds. It had been a gift from a retired cop. The 38 Special had been Art Grulke's service weapon. Art told him that in thirty years on the force he'd never fired the gun at anyone.

Art was in his eighties now, living in a nursing home, and slowly succumbing to diabetes. Sores that wouldn't heal because of poor circulation. First they'd taken off his foot, then they'd amputated above the knee. Last time Jim had visited Art he couldn't feel his other foot and had pressure sores on his butt. Losing his body piece by piece. Poor fucker.

Cops didn't carry guns like that anymore. Five shots couldn't compete when anyone could buy a semi-auto with a fifteen round magazine. Officers he'd seen back in Wisconsin carried Glocks. Ugly sounding name, ugly looking gun.

Jim reckoned the kidnappers had a lot of fire power. He'd be out numbered and out gunned. He told himself he wasn't planning a shootout, he'd get killed for sure. This had to be hit and run. Anyway, if he did get shot it would be a better way to go than poor, fucking Art Grulke.

He wasn't sure exactly what he'd do when they came down the trail. Had to get them to chase him into the trees. Fire some shots and hightail it, sure. But he wondered if he'd be able to really shoot at the men, try to hit them.

The drizzle softened the scenery around them like looking through a misty window. Jim watched droplets of water bead up on Buck's mane and on the nearby pine needles. He breathed in the moist air, a refreshing change from the usually arid air at this altitude. Just as he started to relax a movement across the trail caught his attention. Shit. As he slowly reached for his gun the drizzle stopped and he saw the doe turn and bound back into the trees.

Jim's heartbeat slowed and he tried to settle himself. He gazed into the middle distance, not focusing on any one thing. Aware of everything and nothing, he waited.

Within ten minutes he saw movement. He picked up the binoculars and focused. There they were. One, two, three, four, five, six riders. Chet was in the middle. The last rider was leading the mules. The one rider was still slumped over, obviously hurt and in pain. And no sign of Bob, he'd gotten away for sure.

Jim backed Buck up well into the trees, their view now

straight across the trail. His stomach was in a knot. "Why are they leading three mules, Buck?" he whispered. "It's got to slow them down some. The panniers don't look very full at all. One mule could carry all their gear. Why the extra mules? Huh. Well, they obviously need them for something. If I could get those away from them, they'd chase the mules."

There were only six of them. Where's the other guy? No time to worry about him. If I don't stop them they'll run into those scouts. Got to do this now! They were close. He lowered the binoculars.

The men started to pass riding single file, a mere thirty feet away. The first two riders held a hand gun in one hand and the reins in the other. They were looking around without focus. The horses looked tired, heads down, just plodding along. The men were quiet, none of the complaints he'd heard earlier. Then came Chet. The next one held a rifle. Then came the guy slumped forward in the saddle. Jim reckoned the last guy would have both hands busy, reins in one hand and the lead rope for the mules in the other.

That was his target, the weakest link. Okay, I'm going to do this. He quickly looped the reins over the saddle horn and drew his revolver and cocked the hammer. His hand shook a little so he gripped the gun with both hands. He took a deep breath and blew it out.

The last man was crossing in front of him. He was on a big, gray gelding. The guy had a ball cap on and was wearing a blue windbreaker.

Jim reacted, his brain giving orders without conscious thought. He kicked Buck into a charge and guided him with his legs.

Buck exploded out of the trees, his powerful hind quarters

pumping, throwing dirt and pine needles behind him. Using his legs. Jim steered him directly at the last rider. They were on him in seconds. Just before Buck hit him, the guy looked straight at Jim. Then things seemed to happen in slow motion.

Jim saw the man's eyes widen and his mouth gape open in surprise. His horse shied away from the charging Buck and squealed in alarm. They were very close now. Jim's field of vision narrowed and he couldn't hear anything except the thunder of Buck's hooves. Buck's ears were pinned back, his neck stretched forward. The man dropped the lead rope and started to reach inside his jacket.

Jim saw the movement. He was glued to the saddle and bouncing along with Buck's motion. He held the gun straight out in front of his chest, tried to keep it steady, saw nothing but the man directly ahead. A voice in his head said to aim for center mass. Jim fired at the man's torso then squeezed the trigger again. Jim barely heard the explosions, so intent on what he needed to do.

He saw the man crumple into himself from the impacts and fly from the saddle as the horse reared in panic. Buck dodged the man and the panicked horse turned and ran.

Without looking down at the fallen man or looking at the others, Jim swung Buck toward the mules. The mules had stopped, eyes turned to Buck. Leaning half out of the saddle, he reached over with his left hand and grabbed the lead rope up near the front mule's halter. Jim only had to think "rollback" and shove his feet forward in the stirrups. Buck stopped for a split second and Jim poked his left foot into Buck's flank. Buck pivoted on his hind feet, front feet in the air for an instant, made a hundred and eighty degree turn and blasted back the way they'd come.

Buck kept charging and they sped north into the trees. The horse did not hesitate, just bulled his way into the forest. The mules were too startled to do anything but follow along. Jim let most of the lead rope slip through his hand and tightened his grip when the mules were up to speed.

With the lead rope in one hand and the gun still in the other, Jim bent low in the saddle as they crashed through the trees. Behind him he heard shouts and then gun shots. The men were going to come after him, it was all up to Buck. He trusted Buck to pick a route through the thick growth of pines. He concentrated on holding onto the lead rope. The excited mules followed Buck without detour.

He had no idea how long they raced through the trees and brush and rocks. Everything was a blur of green, pine boughs brushing his legs and shoulders, Buck, moving like a pro half back, was running, dodging trees and boulders, switching leads, pivoting left and right without slowing. Somehow Buck avoided every tree trunk that would have whacked Jim's legs and every low tree limb that would have bashed his head. Everything was Buck's motion, trees whizzing past, the horse's muscles propelling them like a living, breathing locomotive. It was wild, exhilarating. Jim could only glue himself to the horse, become part of the horse, flow with the jigs and jogs and dodges.

Jim lost all sense of time and direction as Buck flew through the forest. Buck finally slowed to a walk and Jim didn't argue. He heard no sound of pursuit. All he heard was loud breathing. Buck's nostrils were flared, the pink inside showing, when he turned his head to look at Jim, his eye bright, excited, pleased with himself. The mules were steaming and blowing. He holstered his gun, realized he was also breathing hard. Looking around, he saw dense pine growth all around him. He didn't see any landmarks in the green gloom under the trees but he knew they were north of the trail and east of the ATV road.

Only then did he think about what he had done. He had shot a man, probably killed him. He felt like he'd opened a door and stepped into a different reality. Jim took a deep breath and blew it out. Then he leaned over and threw up.

Chapter 50

Two gunshots behind him. Fuck! What were those idiots shooting at? Big Jack yanked his horse around, saw the others turning also, all the horses nervous, jittering about on the trail. Ed was on the ground, his horse running down the trail. He saw that damn rock thrower charging into the trees leading the mules.

Fritz jumped down and ran over to Ed. "Jack, he's hurt real bad! He needs help. The mules are gone."

"I know that you idiot. After them. Leave him, there's no help for him. We need the mules, they've got all our gear and food."

"Jack," Botts hollered, "the satellite phone, the mules have it!"

"Go, go, get that fucker!" Jack kicked his horse and went headlong after the thief and the mules. The others followed, bouncing almost out of their saddles as their horses took off.

Fritz looked down at Ed. There was blood oozing from his chest and from his stomach. Ed coughed and blood leaked from his mouth. He looked up at Fritz, eyes pleading. Then he closed his eyes and groaned. Ed started to gurgle. Blood was flowing steadily from his gut. Fritz knew Jack was right, there was nothing that could be done for Ed. He stood there for a moment, realized that his friend was going to die, wondered how it had come to this. "Fuck, fuck, fuck."

He thought about running away but was afraid to be alone in the wild. Without a word, he took the pistol from the dying man's belt, mounted his horse, and rode after the others.

Ed lost consciousness a minute later and died alone in the dirt.

Within a minute, Jack had cracked his knee on a tree and had almost been decapitated by a low branch. He swore at his horse and yanked on the reins. The horse stopped so abruptly that he almost went flying over the horse's head and neck and only just managed to grab the mane to save himself. He groaned, his balls had slammed into the saddle horn. "Shit, shit, shit," he grunted through gritted teeth.

He had to slow down and be smart or he'd run into an ambush himself. Damn it, they needed the mules, the food, the sleeping bags, and that phone. Needed the mules to carry the money. He waited for the others to catch up with him.

"Listen up. We've got to get that bastard. He's going to pay and he's going to wish he'd never crossed my path. And he's killed two of your pals. Spread out and keep going in this direction. Listen for the mules."

Chapter 51

Buck had been startled by the gunshots but he hadn't hesitated to follow his man's directions. The man had given him the reins and used only his legs and feet. Buck knew how to respond and had done so flawlessly. He hadn't hesitated, such was his training and his trust in the man. It was as if the horse's brain was connected directly to the man and the signals to his muscles were almost instantaneous.

Now he was excited to be crashing through the trees and brush leading the mules. Although the mules could be contrary and stubborn, right now they were following without question. Buck had been given his head. Jim had asked him to go and left the route up to him. The horse gave himself over to this mad dash. Yet, dodging and weaving, he was careful to avoid anything that might hit his man or tangle with the mules' panniers.

He felt the mules faltering, their feet getting clumsy, their breathing loud. They would not keep up much longer. Buck let out a big snort and slowed to a walk. He could have kept going full tilt for a while longer but the mules were gasping. His man wanted the mules so he let them stay with him.

Chapter 52

He knew it was best to keep the animals moving at a slow walk so they could cool down gradually. Jim let Buck pick his own path and concentrated on listening for any sound of pursuit. They would be after him but cautious since they knew he was armed. It proved impossible to hear anything over the blowing and snorting of the mules and the thump of panniers against trees and brush. There wasn't anything he could do about it, so he figured he'd just keep moving, stay ahead of his pursuers.

After about a half hour of walking they came to a narrow stream. Jim let the animals drink and he got down. His legs were wobbly from the wild ride. He replaced the bullets he fired. "That's what Spenser would do," he said to himself. He looked over at Buck who raised his head from the stream, water dribbling from the corners of his mouth. "Buck, that was an amazing ride, you're the best." Jim went over and stroked his neck.

Sunlight had begun to slant through the trees; the afternoon was moving toward evening. Jim walked over to the mules and started opening the panniers hoping to find food. He found clothes, damp sleeping bags, and canned food. He kept poking and digging and was rewarded with a small bag of sugar cookies. Upon opening the bag he discovered that the cookies were now crumbs. He helped himself to a handful and then gave another to Buck. It didn't take long for them to empty the bag.

They were both licking their chops when Buck turned to look behind. Buck had heard something. Jim followed the horse's gaze but saw nothing. Then he heard the crunch and clop of a horse approaching. It was close, too close to run for it. He'd have to defend himself.

Jim crouched behind a tree and held his breath. It sounded like only one horse. He drew his revolver. Maybe they'd pass by, if not, he'd wait until the rider was very close to increase the odds of hitting his pursuer.

He looked over at Buck and the mules. Buck was fully alert, eyes staring into the trees, ears pointed forward. The mules appeared unconcerned, nibbling at the sparse grass.

The hoof beats came closer and stopped. The trees were so thick he couldn't see horse or rider. He heard the horse snort. He took another breath, straining his ears for some clue as to where the rider was. Jim raised his gun and searched for a target.

"Don't shoot. I'm unarmed."

Jim knew that voice - "Bob!"

"Yeah, thanks to you I'm on the loose." Bob rode up and let his horse drink with the others. He reached down and shook Jim's hand. "Jim, you saved my life. Thanks. Those bastards were going to kill me sooner or later."

Bob turned in the saddle. "We'd better move on soon, those bastards are about a half mile back. With the racket those mules make in the trees you're not real hard to follow."

Jim mounted up. "Do you have any idea where we are? All I know is that I've been going kind of north."

"I've got a pretty good idea." Bob lowered his voice and looked back. "Let's get somewhere where we can dump this cargo. Follow me, we'll talk later."

As they moved off, Jim asked "how did you find me?"

"I've been tailing those guys ever since you busted me loose with your ambush. I hid in the trees and waited while they sorted things out. Two of the horses ran off and I caught old Ralph here. That was a brilliant idea pelting them with rocks. One of the guys who fell off cracked his head open. They left him there dead. Your ambush was just perfect. You really did save my life. It was the only way I was going to escape."

"Bob, you'd have done the same for me. I knew they'd either kill you when they got down from the mountains or use you as a hostage. I had to bust you out." He shook his head. "But I didn't plan to kill anyone."

"Well you did right. Why the gun play back there? Why steal the mules?"

"I ran into a bunch of boy scouts at Cloud Peak Reservoir. I had to buy them time to hide. I shot the guy leading the mules. I think I hit him twice. I guess I killed him." Jim paused, swallowed. "I figured they needed three mules for something important and they would chase them, or chase me to get even for the ambush. So I led them away from the boys."

"Boy scouts? Oh, brother. You made the right move about the mules. Did you look in the panniers?"

"I looked some. Didn't find anything useful, can't exactly cook canned food with them looking for me."

Bob chuckled. "You took all their gear. They've got nothing to cook. Bastards."

The trees opened up and there in front of them was a small lake.

"Bob, this isn't Gem Lake?"

"Nope, it's called Mud Lake. Too shallow for fish."

The lake was not much bigger than the foundation for a small house and surrounded by boulders. A man would have to climb down to it.

"Let's take a minute and figure out what we're going to do." He looked over at Jim.

Jim was looking at the lake, not really focusing on the still water or the surrounding meadow of grass and wildflowers, both glowing in the late sun.

"Jim, hey Jim. Are you listening?"

Jim blew out a breath. "Sorry," he gulped. "I was thinking." His voice dropped almost to a whisper. "I was thinking about those men I killed."

"Jim, settle down. This is war. Those guys killed Dave and they were going to kill me. Their leader, Jack, is one evil SOB. Keep it together, we're not safe yet. Save the second thoughts for when we're down from here."

This didn't settle things down for Jim at all. He realized that Bob didn't feel sorry about him killing those men. He had a jumble of feelings about what he'd just done, but he needed to push them away, stay focused. Bob was right, they needed to take care of business.

"Okay, here's what I know. They've kidnapped Chet and they're going to wait for the ransom at the reservoir. I heard them talking about ten million dollars. I think that's why they brought all three mules. Ten million in cash is a lot to carry.

They've been using a satellite phone to make their demands. That phone's in the panniers."

"Bob, I've been calling the sheriff. I saw them shoot Dave and told him. After you left camp I freed the family and sent them off to Seven Brothers. I've told the sheriff that they were headed up here. Told him I was going to try to bust you loose."

"I knew you'd take care of the family." Bob smiled. "Good thinking to send them to Seven Brothers, keep them out of the way." He turned serious again. "There's still four of them and they've got another man who's going to cover the trailhead. There's nothing we can do for Chet, we'd only get shot. They won't hurt him until they get the money. I'll fill Zeke in and help him if I can. I'm going to keep the mules away from them. I'm going to head for the ATV road and get down that way to the trailhead. I can't turn these animals loose, no telling what would happen to them."

"So right now we've got the four guys somewhere behind us and another from their bunch between us and our way out. And then there's the boy scouts." Jim shook his head, knew he couldn't leave with Bob. "I've got to get them out of here, move them south past Ant Hill and out that way."

"Jim, I think that's your best way out of here. Get those scouts moving and follow them yourself."

"Yeah, just have to dodge those four guys." Jim blew out a breath. He knew he had to take care of the scouts but it meant he couldn't leave yet.

"I'm going to head due north with these mules. I'll stay off the ATV road as long as I can and try to make it to the trailhead. I'll call the sheriff when I'm well clear."

"I don't know where the sheriff is. He was raring to get

174

up here and something screwed up his plan. When you talk to him tell him I'll call after the scouts are clear of this mess."

"Well, there's not much he can do for us right now. You just be careful and take care of those kids."

"Okay, Bob. Good luck. I'd best get going before dark." And with that, Jim reluctantly started back.

Chapter 53

He stayed in the woods and went around Mud Lake to the west, not risking being out in the open. Hyper alert for any sign of the kidnappers, he scanned all around and strained his ears for any sound. Jim flinched at any noise, as nervous as a pregnant mare. He let Buck pick his way, wending around rocks and trees. He again trusted Buck not to bang his leg into a tree trunk or his head into a low branch. As they walked, the gathering dusk made the already dim light under the trees become gloomier. He strained to peer into the deepening shadows. He kept telling himself to relax, the horse would sense any danger before he could. But he didn't want to give himself time to think about what had happened and what he still needed to do.

It had been a relief to join up with Bob. Another human, a friend, Bob shared the burden of the situation. He'd wanted to talk through what he'd done, but there was no time for that. Now he and Buck were on their own again, roaming the wilderness and dodging the most dangerous predators of all. And he still had the responsibility of getting those boy scouts safely away. All Along the Watchtower ran through his head and he mumbled, "There must be some way out of here." He wondered if he was the joker or the thief.

A short time later Jim heard gun shots from behind, not close. A rapid pop, pop, pop and then another series of shots. He hoped it was Bob doing the shooting.

Chapter 54

Bob heard them coming. It was impossible not to. They made enough racket for three times their number. They were spread out, not going single file, voices, curses, lots of snapping branches, horse shoes clattering on rocks. "Cocky bastards," he muttered.

There was no way he could outrun them with the mules in tow. He dismounted and tied the animals to a couple of trees, leaving the mules still on the string. Then Bob hefted the assault rifle he'd found in one of the panniers and crept toward the noise.

He saw them picking their way through the trees about fifty yards off and a little to the west. It was getting late, the light slanting, the shadows lengthening. He could probably hit one or two of them but he didn't want to hit the horses or Chet.

But he could slow them down. Bob knelt next to a pine tree and let them get a little closer. He was almost invisible under the boughs. When they closed to thirty yards, he fired a burst into the trees about five feet over their heads.

He got the desired result--the men jumped off their horses, scrambling for cover and yelling to each other. Their horses were left untied and unwatched, nervous, looking around. Good. he thought, now scare the horses off.

He fired into the ground in front of one of the horses, dirt and leaves spouting with the impacts. The horse flew off in a panic. Panic is contagious among horses. The others thundered away at a gallop, crashing through the trees and brush, hooves pounding. Soon the horses were out of earshot, long gone. They were probably happy to get away from these men. Bob hoped they'd find their way down to the trailhead, but anyhow they were better off without the men.

Gunshots boomed in the forest. Bullets whizzed over his head. It was time to go. He fired another burst in their general direction and ran back to the animals and untied them. He got on his horse and fired a last burst then trotted off with the mules in tow. "You bastards can walk."

Chapter 55

Davey Hopkins stopped at the edge of the trees and scanned Triangle Park for any sign that the kidnappers were there. The meadow was still in the late afternoon light. The dirt trail ran straight through the grass to the far edge of the park. He sniffed, smelled no horses or mules and no hint of a fire. Davey checked the trees that bordered the rough triangle and saw no indication of man or beast.

Satisfied that the park was empty, he rode in on his big chestnut mare. He halted in the middle of the park and dismounted. While his horse grazed he examined the trail for tracks in the dirt. Finding multiple hoof prints, he followed these to the far end of the park where the slope up to Ant Hill began. There he stopped and stood listening to the small animal noises in the forested slope of the mountain.

Again satisfied, he walked an expanding pattern on both sides of the trail. Ten yards off the trail he stopped and crouched down. He ran his hand through the grass. Chuckled.

His reconnaissance complete, Davey set up a picket line in the trees parallel to the trail and tethered the horse. He unsaddled her and laid out his bed roll nearby. He dug his sat phone out of a saddle bag and called in to report.

"Sheriff, I'm at the park. All quiet."

"Good. Find anything?"

"Yep. That bunch of kidnappers came through on the trail. Had mules with them. Their tracks go up toward Ant Hill."

"You check off the trail?"

"Yeah. One guy walking and leading a horse."

"That would be Jim Taylor."

"He was smart to stay off the trail. It took me some work to find his tracks. Couldn't be seen from the trail."

"No tracks coming back down?"

"Nope. I'm sure."

"Okay. You set up to stay?"

"Yep. Rosie and I are all set. I'll keep you posted."

It was getting on to dusk. Everything was shadow, shades of gray, details fuzzy. He was afraid they'd blunder into the kidnappers. Buck needed a rest. Jim dismounted and let the horse graze while he held the reins. He munched on a couple of granola bars. "Sure getting tired of these, Buck. A hot meal would be heaven. What I wouldn't give for a cup of coffee."

They waited until it was full dark under the trees. The sky was clear so Jim was counting on the light from the stars and the moon. They set off again heading south, Buck's foot falls muffled by the pine needles. Everything not under a tree was bathed in silvery light. They meandered through the light and dark until they came to the trail. On the trail visibility was as good as being under street lights.

Jim recognized where they were, just a quarter mile from the reservoir. He decided to risk a look and turned Buck that

181

way. They walked slowly and right next to the trees so they wouldn't stand out in the moonlight.

When they got to the reservoir, there was no sign of life. Jim let Buck go down to the edge of the overflow stream to drink. He got down and filled his canteen. He looked out at the water. A slight breeze ruffled the water making a million twinkles of silver on the surface of the reservoir. Beyond loomed Cloud Peak and its sisters, faintly lit, blocking out patches of the starry sky, just as they had done for eons.

"Buck, we're never going to find those scouts at night. Let's hole up and start out at first light." Jim led Buck into the trees on the south side of the trail. They found a shallow depression that was screened by trees and settled in for the night. Jim took the saddle and pad off and gave Buck a quick grooming. The horse gave a great sigh and Jim could feel Buck relax the muscles in his back.

He was dead tired. He had pushed himself to the limit mentally and physically. Too tired to think about the events of the day, what he had done, what Buck had done, he just stood with his hand on the horse's back, his mind numb, his limbs leaden.

Buck hung his head, not even grazing. Buck knew to rest when he needed to. Buckling his front legs, then his rear legs, Buck folded himself down onto his stomach. Jim sat down next to Buck and shared a granola bar. The air was chilling down. With the clear sky at this elevation it would probably drop below freezing this night. "Don't take this wrong, Buck, but I'm going to snuggle up here with you to keep warm." Jim bundled himself up in his duster and reclined with his back against the horse. He took a deep breath. Buck's scent was a combination of sweat, manure, and grass. It calmed him and he closed his eyes.

He was bone tired. Every bone and joint and muscle told him that he was flat out done, out of gas, had pushed himself well beyond any rational limit. There was just no energy left. He couldn't stop yawning. No shivers, though, Buck's heat soaked into him. It was like spooning with a lover.

Although sleep came easily enough, it didn't last long. An attack of leg cramps yanked him awake. As soon as he massaged one cramp into a dull ache, another would assault him. His thighs and calves throbbed between cramps. He was even getting cramps where he didn't realize he had muscles--like the top of his foot. It hurt to move; it hurt not to move. The cramps hurt so much, the pain took his breath away. It felt like he was being attacked by an army of taser wielding gremlins. At its worst, he was massaging on two cramps at once with several others of just slightly less intensity waiting for treatment. He wanted to scream but dared not. Finally, exhausted, he dropped back into sleep and left the cramps to fend for themselves.

Buck had laid down next to a human. This was extremely unusual behavior for a horse. A horse on the ground is helpless. To do this right next to a human demonstrated a rare level of trust.

Then his human had returned the trust by doing the same thing. Rather than being unsettled by this it relaxed Buck. It felt good. He sighed and closed his eyes. When he felt that his man had fallen asleep he opened his eyes and went into a semi awake state where he rested yet was able to let his senses warn him of any danger.

When his man stirred and grumbled, he didn't react. He somehow knew that it was harmless.

Buck savored the body heat they generated. He had never experienced this when lying down. By instinct horses avoided this lest legs get tangled if danger caused them to stand up and flee. Buck just knew that his man would never hurt him.

The small creatures of the night did not approach this pair.

Both horse and man were changing.

Chapter 56

Bob had left the kidnappers far behind. The mules were following on the pack line being reasonable, no detours, no pushing each other, no rope snagged around a tree. The pace was slow, the animals had come a long way this day including the climb up Ant Hill. He reckoned they'd hit the road soon, then there'd be a long descent to the trail head. At this pace it would be the wee hours of the morning before they got there.

Bob shifted in the saddle and wondered how Jim was getting along. He had a tall order in leading those scouts safely away from this mess. But Jim had surprised him with what he'd done so far. Amazed him, really, not only setting up the ambush, but also stealing the mules so the scouts could hide. Not bad for a burn out who'd turned up a few weeks ago begging for a job.

A piercing shriek startled Bob and the animals. He knew that noise and it was trouble. The horse and the mules knew it, too, and started prancing and skittering.

Another screaming shriek.

It was more than the animals could tolerate. Their flight

reflex was unstoppable when they heard this sound. Call it instinct or racial memory, they knew what made that noise.

The mules broke free from the lead rope and took off at a gallop. Bob tried to control the horse but it was no use. He just hung on as the horse fled its most feared predator, a mountain lion.

———————————————

The operation was falling apart around him, their whole original plan out the window. Forced to move from the camp, then snow blocking their planned route. And he'd lost two of his men. Now they'd lost the sat phone and all their gear, food, warm clothes, and sleeping bags. Shit. Everything was turning to shit.

Jack looked at his crew. They were huddled around the fire, heads down, bodies slumped, silent. They were exhausted, hungry, thirsty. Everybody but Botts looked beaten. He figured they'd run out on him if they could. Stevens was scared, hugging himself and muttering. He'd have to watch him. Stevens was a blowhard and a weakling, just a spoiled rich guy, his only loyalty was to himself.

And it was cold, cold as he'd ever been. Thank god for the fire. His face, toward the fire, was hot, his back, away from the fire, was freezing. He had only a light jacket over his shirt. He turned around to warm his back side. Jack stared into the darkness. Again he felt exposed sitting by the fire but there was no choice. He doubted that any of them would get any sleep tonight after those inhuman shrieks they'd heard. He wanted a watch kept anyway. Jesus, he hated these mountains.

Tomorrow they would set off on foot. First they needed

to find the horses or mules to carry the ransom. He'd spread everybody out in a search for them. Now he was pleased to have the extra day. They still hadn't made it to the reservoir and needed to scout the area and set up lookout posts. Shit. He needed to talk with Dude Horvath and old man Stevens, but no fucking phone.

Curse the weather, curse the horses, curse the guide and that damn rock man. He'd come to think of the man who had ambushed them three times as a phantom, a creature of the mountains, who could spring up out of thin air to attack and torment them. He had to remind himself that that rock man was flesh and blood, that he would bleed and die like anyone else if only he could catch him.

Who was the rock man? How did he know about them? What was he doing up here? He'd set up that ambush with the rocks that allowed the guide to escape. Was he the missing assistant? Was he a cop? If he had the chance, he'd make the man talk before he killed him.

He had to stay focused on the operation. In the morning they would have to find the trail and the reservoir. They had to succeed. With the money he would set himself up in South America, live like a king. He'd be set for life. Without the money he was screwed. He'd burned too many bridges to ever work security again. And he owed it to Botts and Horvath. He'd talked them into this job, big risks for a big payoff.

They'd pull this off. They would get to that reservoir tomorrow. With or without horses they'd get that money down from here.

A noise woke Davey in the dead of hight. He pulled on his boots and grabbed his rifle. He stroked his horse as he quietly picked his way out of the trees. He heard the noise again, it came from the meadow.

He got to the edge of the trees and raised the gun to his shoulder. Peering along the iron sights he scanned the star lit park. He found the source of the noise.

Chapter 57

He was sitting beside a mountain lake. There was a fishing rod by his side. Boots off, feet in the water, eating a sandwich. Sunlight was sparkling on the water. His hair ruffled by a warm breeze.

The lake was an oval shape. The far end was bordered by a huge cliff. To the left and right were steep slopes of boulders with big clumps of pines interspersed. Where he sat was a sandy beach. The sun was warming his face while the water froze his feet.

Like a video in fast forward, dark clouds came tumbling over the cliff and blotted out the sun. A chill wind blasted his face. It felt like all the ghosts of winters past were coming to get him. He was overwhelmed with a need to flee.

He stuffed his wet, sandy feet in his boots, got up, and ran away from whatever was coming. A gust of wind nearly knocked him over face first. The wind propelled him along as he ran, pushing him, pushing him. He heard a roar overhead. Looking up he saw the tree tops bending and swaying. A hail of pine needles blew past and swirled like a dust devil.

Then everything went white. Snow was blowing past him faster than he could run. It was coating the trunks of the trees in front of him. Now there was a foot or more of snow on the ground. He was struggling up a slope, his feet plowing through the snow and his body bent forward. Somehow he knew that he had to get to the top of this slope or he would be lost, never to be found.

The slope got steeper. He was on his hands and knees now. Still struggling upward. He had gone beyond cold, couldn't feel his body. Then he was at the top.

He was on a ridge about twenty feet wide. The snow was below him. A whole mountain valley full of white with only green tops of evergreens interrupting the white bowl.

He looked to the other side of the ridge. Shades of green, bright sunlight. It was like the exact opposite of the valley he had just left. He looked back to where he had been. Nothing but clouds. The valley was totally filled with thick clouds, opaque. Even the tree tops were gone. A white nothingness had consumed the valley. It would consume him too if he went back.

He saw lightning strike at the far end of the ridge, then the boom of thunder shook the ground. He turned to the other end of the ridge. A deep, bruised purple cloud roiled and crept toward him. He had to get off the ridge. He looked down to the green side. A rocky cliff. About a sixty degree slope all the way down to the valley.

He hated heights. He was afraid of falling or getting stuck without an escape path part way down. He had no choice, he would have to climb down the cliff. He lay down and stuck his head out looking for a route. There was a ledge about four feet down. He lowered himself onto the ledge. It was narrow. He had to hug the cliff to move along it. If he looked down he would fall.

About thirty yards along he came to a cave set in the cliff. He looked in. The man he had shot looked back at him. He was dead but his eyes were staring at Jim. A fly buzzed out of his open mouth.

Chapter 58

It was close to midnight and although the town was quiet, the Sheriff's Office was bustling with regular staff and FBI personnel, keyboards clacking and phones ringing. Zeke and Agent Janns were sitting in Zeke's office when Bob Lundsten walked in. Both rose and Zeke strode over and shook Bob's hand.

"Bob, you're a sight for sore eyes. You okay? Sit down. Get you a cup of coffee?"

"Thanks, Zeke. That would be alright." Bob sank onto the wooden chair with a sigh of comfort and exhaustion.

Without a summons Doris brought in coffee for all. Instead of leaving, she stood in the corner and listened.

"Bob, why don't you tell us what you know. Then we'll ask questions."

"Okay. The kidnappers were taking Stevens and me up to Ant Hill. I convinced them to go there when the pass was blocked by snow. Didn't want them going back to my camp. One hostage was enough."

"Your man Jim sent the family up to Seven Brothers. They're back safe and sound."

"He told me he did that. Happy to hear they're okay. Anyhow…"

"You've talked with Jim?" Zeke stood and leaned over his desk.

"Yep, I'll get to that. Jim set up an ambush on the way up to Ant Hill. Threw rocks at them and the horses panicked. I jumped off and got away. I caught a horse and tailed them to see if Jim got away. The ambush killed one of them when his horse crushed him into a boulder."

"He threw rocks at them?" Agent Janns asked in disbelief.

Zeke just shook his head.

"Yep, it was the perfect thing to do. Caught them jammed up at a switchback. It was all they could do to stay in their saddles."

"Anyhow, after I got up top I heard Jim ambush them again. He told me he did it to buy time for some boy scouts to get hidden. Shot and killed a man and stole the mules. Led them on a chase north into the forest. I met up with Jim and took the mules down to Piney Creek trailhead. On the way I scared off their horses. Last I saw Jim he was heading back south to get those scouts off the plateau. That's all I know."

"Mr. Taylor's killed two of them?" The agent was on the edge of his chair.

"Yes, sir. Told me the killing is eating at him. I think he's pretty shook up about it. He's been in a blue funk this summer anyhow, won't talk about it. But I know him. He's a good guy and he's got that horse with him. He's tougher than he looks and that horse of his is smart. He'll get those scouts out of there. He'll do what needs to be done, count on it."

"Is he stable? Can he protect those kids?" Agent Janns stood and began pacing.

Bob looked at him and then back at Zeke. "Jim saved my life and he'll save those scouts or die trying." His voice was hard, ready to challenge anyone who doubted his friend.

Zeke shook his head at the agent and calmly asked, "Bob, he know his way around up there?"

"Yep. Camped up there with me a few times."

"Tell us about the kidnappers."

"Well, there were four young guys who didn't say much. They called the guy in charge Jack or Big Jack and his helper's name is Botts. Those two are tough. They're killers."

The agent scribbled notes. "The guy in charge was the bald one?"

"Yes, sir. Botts is scrawny with long hair."

"Anything else?"

"Well, they're pretty pissed off right now. They've lost all their food and gear and their sat phone. They're cold and hungry. And on foot, at least right now."

"Thanks, Bob. We'll let you go get food and sleep."

"What are you doing to get Jim out of there? What about Stevens and the ransom?"

"Bob, we can't get close for fear they'll harm Mr. Stevens. I've got two deputies at the bottom of the trail near Soldier Park. The FBI has the Piney Creek trailhead staked out from a distance. We've got to let the ransom go up there." And I've got Davey Hopkins farther up but the FBI doesn't know that.

"Okay, I get it. When Jim calls tomorrow tell him I got out okay. Let me know if I can do anything to help. I'm responsible for Stevens and I owe Jim. Nobody knows that area better than me." He yawned. "I just need a little sleep. I'll be ready to head back up there in the morning."

"Check in with me when you get up. I'll let you know."

"Uh," Bob gave a sheepish grin. "One more thing. There's a mountain lion somewhere at the north end of the plateau. Got my horse and the mules moving pretty good on the way down."

As Bob was leaving the agent got a call on his cell phone. He listened for a few minutes then said, "Okay, good. Let me know when you get through to security. Try the names Big Jack and Botts, see if those ring any bells." He hung up.

Agent Janns looked over at Zeke. "You were right about Stevens. He's got money troubles. There's an IRS lien for back taxes, interest, and penalties. More than I'll make in my lifetime. His house in Florida is in foreclosure. His yacht has been repossessed."

"So he looks good to be a part of this."

"Yes, sir, Sheriff. But we don't know that for sure. We have to play this straight."

"Okay, but I'm going to tell Jim Taylor when he calls."

"Why?"

"I don't want him risking his life trying to help someone who may be guilty, a party to murder in my county."

"You think he might do that?"

"Look what he's done so far. Never would have expected that from a guy who just happened to be there and a darn lawyer at that." Zeke thought that Bob was right, Jim was tougher than he looked. He hoped Jim didn't have to get any tougher.

Chapter 59

The screech of a jay woke Jim. The sky was lightning. He felt warm. He sat up and saw why. Buck had stayed down next to him in the night. Jim nodded to Buck who was looking at him. "Thanks, old friend. You're a great heater. Let's get you saddled and find those boys. Maybe they've got some breakfast to share." He tried to stand up and his legs buckled, knees, ankles, and hips screamed at him. "Ah, man," he groaned. "Buck my legs are shot. You're gonna have to carry me today."

Buck snorted and stood up, stretching out his fore legs then getting a push from his hind legs.

Rather than go back to the trail, they meandered through the trees south of the trail, more or less angling away from the trail. The morning sun slanted down through the gaps in the trees dappling the light brown ground cover with patches of yellow. Mountain Jays scolded as they passed, Buck quietly plodding through pine needles. Both alert for signs or sounds of the scouts.

They'd find the scouts, get them moving, and follow them down the trail from Ant Hill. There was no reason to hang around. Bob was free and the sheriff could deal with the kidnappers. He and Buck would be in town tonight. He tried to ignore the nagging little voice in his head that reminded him that this had been his plan yesterday before they'd met the scouts.

After about a couple of hours of searching, they came upon a large clearing. There the scouts had set up camp. There were at least a dozen pup tents in a circle with a campfire in the middle. Little colored pennants fluttered at the front of each tent.

The scouts were sitting around the fire eating in the morning sun. The boys looked up at them, fresh faced and innocent, and quickly gathered around Jim and Buck. Jim spoke to the leader he'd met the day before. Jim noticed that the scout leader looked like he hadn't slept, eyes bloodshot, face pale, but there was an edge, a spunk to his posture. Jim reckoned he was a good choice for a scout leader.

"Howdy, I'm Jim. I didn't have much time yesterday. Sorry if I yelled at you, but it was vital that you did what I asked. Do you have your whole group with you here, even those boys who were at the reservoir?"

"Yes sir," he replied. "We thought your story was pretty far out, but I called the sheriff and he told me to do whatever you said. Then we heard gunshots. We heard them a couple of times. What's going on?"

"I bet you did. That's what I warned you about. There are killers and kidnappers up here. They were heading for the reservoir and I'm guessing that's where they are now. You've got to get out of here ASAP. You need to pack up now and head east toward the Archer Corral trailhead."

"Okay, we'll start breaking camp."

"Hey, you wouldn't have any coffee would you?"

Jim was not lucky enough for coffee, but he did get a mug of hot chocolate and a baloney sandwich. Buck was a big hit with the scouts. The boys were from St. Louis and most had never been around horses. Buck made the most of his celebrity, nudging boys with his nose, begging for treats. He got several apples in return.

The scout leader got his boys moving, collapsing tents and packing up gear. But even with his urging it took almost an hour to get his troop packed and ready. He got out a map and Jim pointed out the trail down and around Ant Hill. "This is all downhill and switchbacks once you get to Ant Hill. After that it's pretty easy. You can make it out today if you keep moving," Jim explained.

"What about you, mister?"

"I'm going with you as far as the trail. Then I'm going to backtrack a little ways to make sure nobody is on your tail. After that I'll follow you as a kind of rear guard."

"Do you want some of us to help you scout?"

"No way, these guys are armed and they've killed people. The best thing you can do is move out. If you hear shooting close up, I want you to run off the trail and hide in the woods. I need you to hustle. These guys are nasty."

Jim and Buck set off for the trail with the boys following. He gave up trying to stop them chattering and hoped the thick trees would mute the noise. When they got to the trail he saw them off to the east toward Ant Hill. Once the boys had gone about a quarter mile Jim turned Buck toward the reservoir. He reckoned he'd go a half mile or so then turn and hightail it after the scouts. He and Buck would be out of this mess at last.

Chapter 60

Zeke and Agent Janns were marking reference points on the wall map when Sally Carter knocked on the door jamb.

"Sheriff, I've made some progress on those ATVs."

"Come on in, Sally. This is Agent Janns, FBI. I'm sure he's interested, too."

"Okay." She tucked in her t-shirt, red with Pluto wagging his tail. "The manufacturer returned my e-mail. The six ATVs were part of a shipment to a distributor in Rapid City. We have to go through that company to find the retailer, then find out who bought them."

"Or who they stole them from."

"Yes, sir. The distributor hasn't answered my e-mail and no one is answering the phone over in Rapid."

"Shoot. I guess we can call the police over there."

"Hold on, Sheriff," Janns interrupted. "I'll contact our Rapid City field office. They'll track someone down at the distributor. That'll be the fastest."

Chapter 61

It was clear, sunny, and closing in on noon, a faint whiff of pine resin wafted to them as they passed. The air was dry, not a hint of dew on the grass along the trail. They had gone along for about fifteen minutes without seeing or hearing anything. Jim was about to turn around and follow the scouts when Buck stopped and stiffened. He turned his head to the right and perked his ears. Jim turned to look, but not quickly enough.

A man stepped out of the trees pointing a rifle directly at Jim. "Hold up there, buddy," he growled. He was young and looked haggard, face gray and drawn, a few days' growth of whiskers on his grubby face. His clothes were torn. He was about six foot and bulky, broad shoulders, thick neck, big hands holding the rifle. Squinting in the bright sunlight, his eyes kept shifting from Jim to Buck and back.

Jim kept very still and just watched the guy. His pistol was under his duster and snapped into the holster. Unreachable, useless. Shit. Nothing to do but watch and wait, hope for a chance. All three were surrounded by a sudden quiet. Jim could hear every breath and felt his heart thump. He started to sweat in the chill air, his gut clenched, his pulse racing. If the guy fired, he was dead.

The guy just stood there like a statue, gun pointed at him. Jim could see the black hole at the end of the rifle, the muzzle seemed to grow as he watched. He felt himself drawn, being sucked into that hole, knew that death was at the other end waiting to reach out to him in the form of a lead projectile.

He's going to kill me and try to take Buck. The gun is pointed right at me, he can't miss. He's going to shoot. It's all over. There's not a damn thing I can do. What will happen to Buck after he kills me? Buck won't let him get on or he'll throw him off and run away. He can find his way back to the corral. Buck will survive, Bob will see to him.

With those thoughts Jim felt the tension leave his body. He was loose and ready to react to any chance, any opening.

The man stood there. The rifle did not waiver. Jim took a deep breath, thought he'd try to distract him, buy time, get the guy thinking about something besides shooting. He'd read somewhere that if a victim could get his captor to talk and to think of him as a real person, the captor would be less inclined to kill. "If you're looking for food, you're out of luck. I've got nothing but the clothes I'm wearing."

"Shut up. Don't move."

Shit. He's going to do it now. Make it a head shot so it's fast.

The man approached them, rifle steady, eyes on Jim. Jim felt Buck's muscles tense. The horse snorted. "Easy now," the man said. Somehow the guy realized that if he fired the horse would run. He wanted Buck. Then he came right up to Buck, took a hand off his rifle, and reached for the reins.

He'd done the wrong thing for the right reason. He was about to pay for his mistake.

This was Jim's chance and he grabbed it. With the speed

of thought his brain sent messages and instructions to his muscles. Before his conscious mind could articulate what the body was doing, Jim pushed his right leg into Buck's flank while moving his left leg away and at the same time twitched the reins to the left. The moves were subtle and quick. He was telling Buck to spin, pivot his whole body on his hind legs.

Buck was incredibly fast to react, his response so immediate, it was as if he was connected directly to Jim's brain. He spun to the left, forelegs crossing rapidly, pivoting on his hind feet, and in a blur of speed came around in a full circle.

Buck's head slammed into the side of the man's head with a resounding thwack.

A horse's head weighs at least a hundred pounds and just a slight twitch can smart. Buck's head had the full momentum of the spin. Upon impact the man's skull fractured and he lost consciousness. He flew backwards with the momentum, limp like a rag doll, dropped the rifle, and flopped to the ground five feet away, his head striking a rock. There was a thunking noise like knocking knuckles on a ripe melon.

Jim looked down. There was blood on the rock and blood on the man's head. The man didn't move, not a twitch, his mouth hanging open without a sound coming forth. He knew the man was dead. Jim fought the urge to vomit, closed his eyes and took a deep breath.

Jim jumped down, grabbed the rifle, and swung back into the saddle. He turned Buck back toward where the scouts had gone and they loped off for a quarter mile. Then they stopped. Both Buck and Jim were breathing hard. Jim reached down and patted Buck on the neck. "Jesus, you just saved my life."

Buck turned his head and looked back at Jim, his eye unreadable.

Jim nodded at Buck. "Yeah, we had to do it." He blew out a breath. "Ah, man, I just don't know."

Buck gave a low groan and then snorted. He turned his head to look at Jim as if to say "I'd rather be in my home pasture getting fat."

Buck had never harmed a human before. He had sensed the danger in that man, a threat to his man. When his man had asked him to spin, Buck had done it just as he had been trained to do, his muscles programmed to respond to the signals. He was surprised when he hit the man as he came around. No one had ever asked him to do that, but he did it because his man wanted him to.

He was happy to race away from the downed man. He had smelled blood, sensed death. He did not want to be near. Then his man had thanked him.

Chapter 62

The squad car blocked the gravel access road where it joined the state highway. The test drilling site at Flat Top Mountain was hidden from view four miles along the road. The deputies stood well to the rear of the car watching the protesters.

The protesters were clumped in various sized groups behind a split rail fence that paralleled the highway about thirty yards back from the pavement. Small pine trees and wildflowers dotted the grassy strip where the people had gathered. Most were standing but some sat or lay on blankets. Save for the protest signs and banners the scene resembled a holiday picnic.

The protesters were an odd mixture of local hunters and guides, Save The Earth! activists, and an assortment of people, young and old, with no particular affiliation. Some waved signs, placards, and banners, others just chatted quietly. Also present were a television camera crew and a couple of print reporters.

Although the protesters were peaceful, the deputies were nervous. Zeke Thomasen had pulled four of their colleagues the night before to assist with the kidnapping situation. The remaining deputies felt overwhelmed by the numbers they faced, this day close to a hundred. They knew that if the protesters decided to rush the two of them, they would be unable to stop them from moving on to the drilling site.

The deputies stiffened as a group of about a half a dozen broke away from the crowd and approached. Before either man could raise a warning hand the windshield of the car exploded followed by the boom of a rifle shot. Both dove to the ground as a second shot tore into the hood of the car.

The protesters were slower to react. Several screamed, others shouted. First a few and then the rest ran away down the highway in panic. Placards and posters were strewn over the now deserted road.

Three hundred yards away Dude Horvath grinned then rose from his hide. He slung his rifle on a shoulder. Mission accomplished, he started the hike back to his truck.

Chapter 63

After they had both caught their breath and gathered up their nerve, Jim turned Buck into the trees to the south of the trail. "Buck, that guy was one of the original six. That means there are only three left. If that guy was any yardstick, they've lost their horses and are in fairly rough shape. But they're still armed."

Jim took out the binoculars and scanned the trail and the edge of the woods on the north side. He reckoned if one guy could pop out of the woods and surprise them, then one of the other three could do that, too. He didn't fancy risking that. They'd stay where they were and watch. The scouts would be getting close to the start of the descent down Ant Hill. They'd be safe, but he and Buck were too exposed to follow them. If there was another killer in those trees, he could nail them.

Jim got down and let Buck graze. He checked over the rifle he had taken from the dead man. Bolt action with a clip underneath. A round in the chamber. Unknown if there were any rounds left in the clip. He let it fall to the ground. He had no use for it. The rifle was for hunting. He wasn't about to hunt the remaining men. Didn't want anything to do with them. He just wanted to be far away from there and that wasn't happening. He was a poor shot. His old 38 was strictly for emergencies, a close range weapon. He wasn't a hunter, had never shot anything except trapped raccoons. He'd be a fool to get into a shooting match with the killers, a dead fool.

Where the hell was the sheriff? Where the hell was the cavalry? It felt like he was in an old western movie and he wanted out of it. Those guys were really dead. He'd killed them. He told himself he couldn't dwell on that now. He'd have to deal with that later. He had to think ahead and move forward.

Buck kept on grazing.

They waited under the trees until the sun was directly overhead. Jim munched on baloney sandwiches, courtesy of the scouts. He'd always liked bologna. The sandwiches reminded him of bagged lunches in grade school. As a kid he'd had a fertile imagination but had never fantasized about anything like what he'd been living these past few days. Back then it was just jet fighters, Steve Canyon, stuff like that. Jeez, Steve Canyon. He had a flash of the swing set next to the grade school in Neosho, Wisconsin. Fifth grade, after school, waiting for the bus. Swinging as high as he could, pretending to be flying a jet fighter.

Yeah, he'd had a busy imagination. Probably because he was, what they'd call these days, a nerd. Too fat and slow to be good at sports. Always the last one picked when teams were divided up. Only excelled at academics. Fantasy was his escape.

Anyway, baloney was a pleasant change from granola bars and candy. He fed Buck another apple. The horse drooled apple juice on his chin and smacked his lips.

They watched the world from the shadows. The pine trees, dark green, some with globs of moss hanging down. Deer grass in bright green clusters. Brown and orange pine needles. No flowers or paintbrush as there had been lower down the Solitude Trail and Bob's camp. The air was still, not even a whisper of wind in the tree tops. The sky was that deep, deep blue Jim had only seen in the mountains at higher elevations.

After the flurry of action the woods seemed strangely quiet. Other than an occasional bird call the only noise was Buck nibbling on the sparse grass. Jim sat spread legged, idly picking up bunches of pine needles and flicking them into the air.

He thought of fishing. Flicking a fly into a stream. Sun sparkling on the water making him squint. A quick strike and he had a trout fighting on the end of the line. Bringing it to shore, wetting his hand to gently unhook it and release it. The rich colors of the rainbow. How cold the fish was and yet so alive.

They just enjoyed the quiet contemplation, not thinking about the danger that lurked somewhere nearby. For a time, nothing and nobody else existed but these two friends and the wilderness around them. This hiatus would soon end.

Chapter 64

Feet upon his desk, chair tilted back, Zeke was
taking a nap when his desk phone rang. He woke
instantly.

"Thomasen."

"Sheriff, you'd better come over here to dispatch."

He strode down the hall and poked his head into the
dispatcher's cramped office.

"Sheriff, Parker and DeSmet called in from the protest.
Shots fired, no injuries."

"Get them on the radio."

"Can't. Their squad car got shot up. They called in on a
cell phone."

"Damn. All right. Call them. Tell them to hold tight, I'm
on my way."

"Yes, sir."

"Wait. Is Jerry still at that crash on the interstate?"

"Just wrapping it up."

"Have him meet me there."

Zeke stopped his car on the state highway fifty yards short

of the access road. All the protesters were gone, the media, too. As he walked over to his deputies a few cars passed him on the highway. The deputies were standing out on the shoulder of the highway screened from the access road by a stand of pines.

"You boys okay?"

"Yeah, Sheriff. A little nervous but hanging in there."

"Tell me what happened?"

Parker and DeSmet took turns relating the incident.

"So none of the protesters was near?"

"Right."

"And you were how far away from the squad?"

"About twenty feet, give or take."

Zeke walked up to the car. He focused on the hole in the hood and tried to line up the direction the shot had come from. In the distance were several small rises a sniper could use. Then he scanned behind toward the highway.

He stood next to the car, deep in thought. He looked down at the marks his deputies left when they dove for cover, then glanced at the fallen protest signs. The shooter had a clear line of fire at plenty of human targets. Why shoot the squad car? He had a good enough angle to hit the deputies when they were on the ground. The protest had been peaceful up to now. Why now when he was pulling men to deal with the kidnapping? Who knew about the kidnapping?

Ten minutes later he walked back to his deputies.

"I've got Jerry on his way here. When he gets here I'll give you a ride back to town. Jerry will park on the highway just to keep cars moving. We'll send a wrecker up for your squad."

"You're not going to send more men?"

210

"Nope. I reckon the shooter wasn't trying to hit anyone. Those shots were deliberately aimed at your car. I think he wanted me to send more men, tie them down here so they couldn't help on the kidnapping."

Zeke knew this was a gamble but he needed manpower for the kidnapping. Whoever planned the kidnapping wanted him running around in circles. He wasn't biting on this bait.

Chapter 65

Buck walked up behind Jim and nudged him in the back with his nose. Then he rested his chin on his man's shoulder. Jim reached up and gently stroked Buck between the nostrils. He sighed and shook himself.

"Buck, it's so peaceful right here, right now. For a moment I forgot we're in the middle of a nightmare. We can't just vegetate here forever. Let's take a look see toward the reservoir and the road. If the other three are there then maybe we can follow the scouts after all."

Jim turned around and tightened Buck's girth. The horse grunted.

They walked slowly westward keeping about fifteen to twenty yards away from the trail. The ground gradually sloped downward and the trees were taller and thicker as they got closer to the reservoir. The woods became darker, the light diffused, greenish, like being deep under water. After about an hour and a half, they came to the junction of the trail and the ATV road.

Jim had Buck creep forward to the edge of the trees. The transition from the pine forest to the road was abrupt, from dark green murk to brilliant mountain sunshine. A slight breeze blew across the reservoir making the water sparkle, a million golden flashes pulsing. Jim had fished it in years past. Used a spinning rod and a Jakes lure. On the right day a guy could catch his limit of trout in short order. Other times he could lose lure after lure in the rocks and come away with nothing.

The rocky shore was deserted, the boulders in sharp contrast of sun and shadow. There was no one on top of the dam. All was quiet except for the whisper of the breeze and the lapping of the water on the rocks. At the junction of the trail and the road there was no sign of the kidnappers. They both took a quick scan in all directions, saw nothing but trees, rocks, and dirt. Bob said they'd get the ransom here. Where were they?

The air was so dry up here that the moisture from yesterday's rain had already evaporated. The ground was totally dry and the pine needles crunchy. The sparse grass did get greened up, however. Buck nibbled while Jim watched the junction. The snow from the first night was just a distant memory. Everything smelled dry as if even the ground had been toasted.

Buck pricked his ears and looked to the north on the ATV road. Cautious, Jim backed Buck into the trees to watch, not knowing whether what was coming was friend or foe.

Within a minute, Jim heard the noise too – small engines, ATVs. "Here we go again, Buck," he whispered. Soon the ATVs were in sight. Jim had Buck back up farther to where they could watch but were invisible from the junction. As the machines approached they could see more detail. Two of them, one man on each with a load of gear strapped on the back of the machines. They stopped at the junction and dismounted.

The two men were dressed in baggy pants, fishermen's vests, and ball caps. Were these reinforcements for the kidnappers? Was this the ransom? As Jim watched, one of them took a long tube from the back of the machine and walked toward the reservoir. He set one end on the ground and pulled something out. Some kind of gun? Jim grabbed his binoculars and got a better look. It was a fly rod! These guys were just fishermen.

These guys had blundered into the wrong place. He should warn them. Jim was about to call out to them when Buck quickly turned his head toward the woods along the road. Jim saw movement. Four men walked out. One of them was big and bald. "Oh shit," he hissed.

The four casually walked over to the fishermen, Chet sauntering along like the others. There was some talk but Jim was too far away to make it out. Chet and one of the kidnappers were looking at the gear strapped on the four wheelers. It looked like a friendly visit, just a chit chat by a fishing spot.

What was with Chet? He wasn't acting like a kidnap victim, a hostage. Jim thought back to the day before. When the group was riding nobody was guarding Chet, he was just riding along like he belonged.

Now, with his captors chatting up the fishermen, it would be easy for Chet to make a run for it. He could dart into the trees and be lost to his captors in fifty yards. So what if they saw him run, they weren't going to shoot him before the ransom was delivered. Maybe Chet was just a chicken shit. Huh. Maybe not. Was he part of it?

The bald guy was standing next to the man with the fly rod, as casual as could be. Jim wanted to shout out a warning, tell the fishermen to run for it. But it would be a useless gesture. There was no way the fishermen could escape. Anything Jim did would just get him shot at. A short guy with long hair seemed to be chatting with the other one. As Jim watched, the bald guy and the short guy looked at each other. Both pulled out pistols.

The bastards were going to kill them. He shook his head thinking of what was going through the fishermen's heads. All set for a glorious day of fishing and now held at gun point. Totally out of the blue. Life had gone from sugar to shit.

There was nothing he could do but wait for what he feared would happen. The fishermen had their hands up. The guy with the fly rod was backing up toward the reservoir. Jim could see his mouth move. Beyond them the water sparkled in the sun watched over by the distant peaks. "No, don't do it," he muttered. "Just let them go."

The bald guy gestured with his gun. The fishermen knelt, hands on heads. Ah, geez. "Tie them up, tie them up. You don't have to kill them."

Seconds passed. Jim began to hope.

Boom. Boom. Man and horse flinched. The gun shots echoed from across the reservoir. The fishermen were on the ground. The bald guy stood over his victim, pointed his pistol at the body. Boom.

"Ah, fuck. Jesus." Jim swallowed. His hands were shaking. Buck turned to look at him, a question in his eye.

Buck had made the connection between the bald man's actions and the smells of blood and death.

"Buck, let's get out of here." Jim wanted to be far away. As they started to back away they heard the engines start up again. One ATV took off toward Ant Hill and the other went down the road. "Ah, shit. There went both our escape routes."

Chapter 66

Zeke and Agent Janns were fine tuning the placement of men and the timing of moves for the next day when Doris interrupted with a gentle rap on the door jamb.

Zeke turned. "Yes, Doris?"

"Sheriff, there's two TV vans outside in the parking lot and a bunch of reporters. They're starting to draw a crowd." She walked over to the window. "Take a look."

Zeke joined her and groaned. He looked over at the FBI man. "You've taken control here, you better deal with this."

Janns shook his head. "It's probably about the shooting at the protest. That's your baby. I don't want the media interfering with the kidnapping, so don't mention it."

Zeke grunted and walked out of the office.

———

Zeke stood on the landing outside the front door of the department. He took a minute to scan the crowd. And it was a crowd. One TV crew was from Rapid City, the other from Billings. Each had a reporter, a camera man, and a sound man. Jostling for position were a gaggle of print reporters including Alf Jacobson from the Bison Banner.

The media people were hemmed in by a crowd of spectators. Zeke recognized most of them. Shopkeepers, a mechanic from the Cenex Coop, bar patrons, housewives, and some of the local people from the protest. Sliding through and among the adults were kids, faces bright with excitement, and teenagers trying to look cool and disinterested. Damn, he hated public speaking.

The woman from Rapid City, a perfectly styled blond in a navy pant suit, stepped forward, her sound man following in lock step.

"Sheriff Thomasen, is it true that you pulled some of your deputies from the Flat Top protest? Do you think this encouraged the sniper?"

Zeke was ready for this.

"Our resources have been strained to the limit. In addition to the protest we have an obligation to protect the rest of Flint County. I only have so many deputies and I can't neglect the safety of our citizens by having all my people at the protest."

He paused, thought that came out pretty good.

"At this time we don't believe that the number of deputies at the protest had anything to do with what happened."

Before the woman could ask a follow up question, Alf Jacobson spoke.

"Zeke, is it true that you pulled men from the protest because of the kidnapping in the mountains?"

Oh, shit. Somebody let the cat out of the bag.

Everyone was shouting questions at him now. Chaos.

"Who's been kidnapped? Where did it happen? Is there a ransom demand? How much ransom. . . ?"

217

He had to say something to put them off.

"We are cooperating with the FBI on a matter. I'm sure that a representative will issue a statement soon. I can't tell you more than that." Good grief, I sound like a politician.

Zeke turned and walked back into the building ignoring the shouted questions.

Chapter 67

They back tracked about a half mile and halted. Jim had been too stunned to think. He knew he had to do something and he needed to be far away from that bald headed bastard. They couldn't take the trail to Ant Hill. That route was totally blocked by the guy on the ATV. There was a long open stretch just before the descent. They'd be sitting ducks. North then. They could go through the forest a long ways. He had to believe that the guy who went that way would stop somewhere. If they could get past that point then they could get on the road and get to the trailhead.

Jim walked Buck up to the edge of the trail. He got down and poked his head out, looking both ways. No sign of the men. He mounted up and they walked out of the trees and onto the trail. He had Buck walk very slowly to minimize the noise of his hooves. It seemed to take forever to cross the thirty feet to the trees on the north. Jim kept looking in both directions, scanning constantly. Then they were under cover of the trees. He breathed. He hadn't noticed that he'd been holding his breath.

It was getting late in the day and the gloom under the trees was deepening. They wouldn't be able to make it out until morning. They'd need a place to sleep, but they might as well put more distance between them and the reservoir. Jim let Buck pick his way. He didn't pay attention, sickened by what he'd just seen and frustrated about spending another night in hiding. After about an hour they came to a clearing.

It looked familiar.

It was Gem Lake. He knew this spot pretty well having camped here with Bob in years past. A meadow about a hundred yards wide ran east from the small lake up a gentle hill. Grass grew thick on the meadow sprinkled with wildflowers, little bits of red, yellow, and white in the sea of green. It was bordered on three sides by thick forest. To the east the meadow abruptly ended in a steep rock fall of a thousand feet.

It was getting on to dusk. Time to stop and set up for the night. This was a good place, Jim felt safe here. "Hey, Buck, let's look around a little. Maybe Bob cached some things from his camp."

Jim got down and let Buck graze. He walked over to where Bob had set up a picket line for horses the last time he was here. The ground was worn bare from the horses with manure spread all around. Jim nosed a bit at a big fallen log. Under the log was a tarp.

He pulled up the tarp. "Buck, we got lucky. Come on over here." Inside the tarp was a fifty pound bag of horse cubes, a tin of biscuits, and a six pack of Coors.

Buck came trotting over. Jim dumped out a pile of cubes for him and grabbed himself a beer. "As my grandmother used to say 'the condemned ate a hearty meal.' Eat up and then I'll take you down to the lake for a drink." He took a big swig of beer. He couldn't taste it, but it felt like it might wash away some of the foulness.

As he sat drinking, Jim remembered the sheriff. He got the cell phone and called.

Chapter 68

Sheriff Zeke Thomasen watched as the scouts were loaded onto a bus. He gave a silent thank you to Jim Taylor for preventing what would have been a disaster. *Where are you, Jim? Why didn't you follow the scouts? Are you even alive?*

Zeke looked around the Archer trailhead. Dust swirled, kicked up by the bus as it left for town. Half a dozen squad cars and pick-ups and a couple of horse trailers were parked haphazardly near the corrals. Bob Lundsten was saddling two horses. He and Zeke would head out in a few minutes to meet up with the deputies at Triangle Park. Other deputies would come up in the morning. In the west the sun was about to slide down past the mountain peaks. They would finish their ride in the dark.

A deputy came up. "Sheriff, the FBI is on the radio. Wants to talk to you."

Zeke walked over to the squad. "Thomasen here."

"Sheriff, Agent Janns. We're all set up near Piney Creek trailhead. I've got three agents watching. They'll work in shifts through the night. We're about a mile away and screened by an abandoned barn."

"Anybody at the trailhead?"

"Yes, sir. A fellow in a big van pulling a trailer with an ATV on it. He's been sitting there for a couple hours. Just sitting. I figure he's with the kidnappers, probably going to make sure no one follows the ransom up the trail."

"Did Stevens Senior, confirm the time for us?"

"Yes, ten a.m. the ransom starts up the trail."

"Any luck with West Slope security?"

"Finally. The chief of security has gone off on some errand, but I spoke with his assistant. Our suspects are Jack Bulganin and Joseph Botts. Worked for West Slope as security until about a month ago. Both ex-special forces and ex-Mideast security contractors."

"Are you thinking what I'm thinking?"

"Yes, but we have no proof, yet."

"Yeah, I know. I'm moving in closer tonight. We'll start the climb up tomorrow."

"Don't be too early."

"I won't, but I'll be close and ready to move in on your signal."

"Any word from that man Taylor?"

"No. He was with the scouts this morning. That's the last we know."

"Thank God for him getting those scouts out. I don't want to think about what tomorrow would be like if they were still up there."

"Amen to that." Zeke blew out a breath and straightened his shoulders. "Alright. I'm going to head out now. If you need to call me relay the call through my dispatch. They can reach my cell phone."

As Zeke walked over to the horses his cell phone rang. He was tired of talking, wanted to get moving. "Thomasen."

"Sheriff, Jim Taylor."

Zeke waved Bob over, whispered, "He sounds rough. Listen in."

"Jim, where are you? Why weren't you with the scouts?"

"Figured I better be a rear guard, get them off safely. I ran into some trouble. They okay?" Jim was almost whispering.

"Just fine. On a bus going to town. Bob's here with me."

"Good. Look, Sheriff, I stayed behind. I was going to follow them but I got jumped by one of the kidnappers. I killed him. Did Bob tell you about the other two I killed?"

Zeke looked at Bob and shook his head, mouthed "He's shaky." "Yep, said you saved his life."

"I'm sorry, Sheriff. I guess you're going to have to arrest me when this is over." Jim's voice was soft, his words slow. "I've never even hurt anyone before. Now I've killed three men. I'm sorry."

Zeke grimaced, thinking fast, got to help this guy pull himself together. "Jim, you did what you had to do. Besides, I deputized you that first night, just forgot to tell you. As a deputy you're entitled to use deadly force." Bob gave Zeke a thumbs up.

"Well, I've had enough of it. I'm too fucking good at it. I want out of here, but I'm stuck." His voice was hoarse, tired. "These guys just killed two fishermen at the reservoir. Just executed them. Took their ATVs. One guy went toward Ant Hill, the other went down the ATV road. Must be lookouts. I'm at Bob's camp at Gem Lake." He paused. "We just wandered to the north hoping to get to the trailhead somehow. I may be trapped. How do I get out of here?"

"Things will happen tomorrow. The ransom is going up there at ten a.m. from Piney Creek. All that money will keep them occupied and you can sneak off then." Zeke was being upbeat, trying to exude confidence. "I'll be coming up Ant Hill. The FBI is at the other trailhead. And don't worry about Stevens, I think he's in on this."

"No shit? Well, that bald guy is a stone killer. Chet had better watch himself."

"We'll see to that. You just hold tight and be ready to move. Meet us at Ant Hill. We'll ride out together."

"So I wait until ten?" Jim sighed.

"Yep. Then you'll be good to go."

"Wonderful." Jim did not even try to hide his disgust.

Jim rang off. Zeke turned to Bob. "You hear him okay? What do you think?"

"Zeke, we've got to get him out of there. He's about had it. You heard it in his voice. Jim's killed three men. It's doing things to his head."

"We're stuck until tomorrow. He's got to hang on. He's at Gem Lake, so he's out of danger. Jim just has to stay clear until those bastards make their move for the ransom."

"That's not what I'm worried about. Those killings are weighing heavy on him. Telling him he was deputized was brilliant. I'm sure that helped. I know Jim, it's his conscience that's eating at him." He looked over at Zeke. "You ever killed a man?"

Zeke nodded. He had a far away look in his eyes. "I did. Long ago. Still bothers me. Not something I like talking about. Let's get going."

They mounted up and rode into the gathering dark.

Zeke remembered all too well. He'd only been sheriff for

225

a few months. A Saturday night in mid-summer. Rance Windig was a young ranch hand. Zeke learned later that Rance had lost his job and his girl on the same day. He'd gone into town to drown his sorrows.

At two in the morning Zeke had been sitting in his office waiting for his deputies to return from a crash on the interstate. He heard gun shots through the screen window and bolted out the back door. As he trotted down an alley he had realized he had no backup.

When he got to Main Street he saw, starkly lit by street lights, the young man standing in the middle of the street with a rifle in his hands. Half a block down the street bar patrons had spilled out of the Lucky Star, at least a dozen, drinking and shouting encouragement. As Zeke watched, Windig howled and fired at a store front then staggered a few paces and fired again.

Reluctantly Zeke drew his pistol. He hated what was coming but had no choice. The odds were that someone would get shot. The next minutes were clear in his memory despite the passage of years.

"Son, this is the Sheriff. Drop your weapon and come with me."

Windig turned toward him and pointed his rifle at Zeke.

"Drop your rifle. I'll put you in a cell and let you sober up. Whatever wound you up is not worth dying for." Zeke did not want to shoot this kid. He said a silent prayer that he would sober up enough to back down.

"No fuckin' way. There's no fuckin' thing left to live for. I'm gonna to shoot up this stinkin' town," Windig slurred. He belched and let out another howl. He stood swaying directly under a street light.

Zeke still had the vivid image in his mind. The young man was dressed in his going to town clothes, new jeans, white snap button shirt, black felt hat.

Zeke walked closer.

"Son, if you don't drop the rifle now I'm going to have to shoot you."

"Fuck you, Sheriff. I don't care." Windig fired a wild shot in Zeke's direction.

Fifteen feet away Zeke dropped to one knee next to an old red GMC pick-up. "Please don't make me do this."

Windig fired again, hitting the truck, shattering a side window.

Zeke raised his weapon and fired. The bullet hit the young man in the chest. Blood blossomed on the white shirt, looking black in the harsh light. Rance Windig collapsed in the street.

By the time the ambulance responded he was dead.

Chapter 69

After watering Buck, Jim led him over near the rock fall. He took his saddle off. Buck folded himself down and rolled onto his back, legs and feet straight up in the air, rubbing like a person would rub his back against a wall. Jim sat on a rock and watched. He looked off to the east. They were a little above 10,000 feet, about 6,000 feet above the plains below. From this height, the view was spectacular. In daylight he remembered seeing at least a hundred miles or more. Now he watched darkness slowly creep across the plains and approach the mountains. Lights came on in town twenty miles away. In the distance, he could see the lights of a larger town, probably Gillette. He watched the wooded foothills disappear into deepening shadows. The darkness crept up the rock fall, the boulders and scrub pines losing their shapes. Then man and horse were swallowed by the oncoming night.

Jim cracked another beer and opened the tin of biscuits. Stale but better than what else he had to eat which was nothing. He looked up at the stars, the millions and billions of stars. He could almost hear Carl Sagan. The sky was just so full of stars. Billions more than could be seen back in civilization. The black between the stars seemed blacker and deeper, endless. He tried to imagine what it would be like to voyage into that endless night. He wondered if those dead men had souls and if they did, were they out there in that eternal blackness.

He thought about all the deaths in the past few days. First Dave, the sudden shock of it, then his own ambushes, three deaths on his head. And then those two fishermen at the reservoir. How that bald guy fired a second shot like an execution. "Judas Priest. Buck, it has been a slaughter up here. Bodies all over the place." He groaned. "Am I any different from the bastards who shot Dave and those fishermen?"

Buck nuzzled his neck and snorted into Jim's hair.

Jim reached up and stroked Buck's face, thankful for his companionship. They sighed in unison. Both relaxed, comfortable in this safe place, comfortable with each other.

Jim continued to stare off to the east. Thought about all he'd left behind, family, friends, his business, partners, clients, opponents. His past. All the people he knew going about their daily lives, no one aware of what he and Buck had been through. All this would never be real for them, just a story he could tell.

He grimaced. He didn't want to resume that life. The responsibilities and worries were slowly killing him. Going back meant more of the same. He'd had enough of that life. That was why he was here. He wondered if this had given him some kind of subconscious death wish that had led him to do the things he'd done the past few days. If he lived through this he'd take it as a reason to stay here. He grunted.

He drifted into thoughtlessness, just looking into the darkness, hearing the wind in the trees and Buck cropping grass. It was rest and peace. In my office back in Wisconsin I have a wall full of diplomas and certificates. Those mean nothing here. What was that line by the Airplane? 'Da, da, da, da, da, da, a human name doesn't mean shit to a tree.'

"Buck, this business with the killers has certainly simplified my world view. I'm either scared shitless, starving, or exhausted. Sometimes I'm all three. At least I've got good company."

Buck snorted and continued grazing.

He was so lucky to have Buck with him. Most of the horses Jim had ridden up in the mountains were what he would call worker bees. They did their job without question and that was pretty much all there was to them. They showed no inclination to be friendly with humans and no curiosity about anything. They were totally reliable but had no personality. Their only animation was about food. That and going back to the corral where they knew they wouldn't have to work.

Bob's mules, on the other hand, all had individual personalities. They did their jobs, of course, but they seemed to enjoy interacting with humans. Jim remembered one little roan mule named Jake. Jake would roam the camp untethered. At meal time he would come up to the cook tent to cadge treats. He especially loved pancakes and would get half his body into the cook tent begging for those. Another special little mule was Festus. His full name was Festus T. Hagen, after the character in the T.V. show Gunsmoke. His favorite treat was Ritz crackers. When he knew there were Ritz crackers to be had he would get so excited that he would prance and sway.

The horses he had back on his farm had personalities and quirks. He didn't think he was projecting onto them or anthropomorphizing. Maybe he'd encouraged them a bit. Certainly living with the horses allowed humans to be more aware of their personalities. Some horses definitely showed more interest in humans than others.

Jim thought Buck was in a class by himself. He was an accomplished reining show horse but was not aloof at all. He was extremely friendly to humans as well as other horses. Some of this was probably due to the show circuit regimen. Show horses did not really get to hang out and play with other horses. They were worked and trained daily and then, when turned out, they were put into barren paddocks by themselves. The one interaction they had was with humans.

Buck seemed exceptionally intelligent and perceptive. He was also playful with humans and extremely curious. Yet he was all horse and loved to run and frolic and graze. Perhaps what struck Jim the most was the look in Buck's eye. Buck said a lot with his eye. He was also quite vocal and had an interesting range of sounds. He believed that Buck understood a lot of what was said. The horse was perceptive and intuitive, almost as if he could read minds. He loved the horse.

He looked over at Buck. As far as he was concerned Buck was the ideal horse. Ancient Greeks such as Plato and Aristotle held that material things and beings were just imperfect manifestations of abstract, pure, ideal forms. As in Plato's cave, Buck would just be a shadow of the form "horse."

Huh. What was the essence of "horse?" Graceful movement, speed, power? DNA maybe? No, none of this accounted for the personality of a horse, the heart and courage and loyalty that a horse such as Buck had demonstrated these past few days.

Jim sighed. Their ordeal was almost over. They would leave together in the morning.

Chapter 70

He stopped and killed the engine. He listened for a few minutes to be sure he was alone then hid the dirt bike in the bushes. The man knelt in the grass and spread the map out. Checked his compass to orient himself. Gazed up at his route.

He checked the scoped rifle and put it back in its case. Dropped the clip from the 9mm and dry fired it. Satisfied, he reloaded and snapped it back into his shoulder holster.

He settled down to wait.

When it was full dark he shouldered his gear and headed off. He had several miles to go and it was rough country. He needed to get in position before first light.

Only small night critters noted his passage.

Chapter 71

His stomach grumbled reminding him about hot food. Bacon, sausage, ham, eggs, and a big pile of American fries. Man, he loved American fries. He had a mental list of the restaurants that had the best yanks. The truck stop in Nodine, Minnesota, just a few miles west of the Mississippi River, never failed him. The Pioneer Restaurant in Westfield, Wisconsin, was a close second. His stomach grumbled again. His clothes felt loose, Jim wondered how much weight he'd dropped since this ordeal had begun.

It struck him that his preoccupation with food, especially the hot variety, was an indication of the immediacy of his existence right now. He was used to eating when he was hungry and having hot coffee available whenever he wanted it. That was life in civilization. There were no convenience stores or diners in the wilderness of course, but there was always food and drink available at Bob's camp.

Now even that vestige of normalcy had been stripped away. He could not take food for granted. Now warm beer and stale crackers were a treat to be savored. He felt almost giddy. Food was a constant concern. There were other things, too, which he always took for granted.

"Buck, you just smell like yourself. Need some serious grooming, but you smell of horse. Me, I have some of your smell on me and quite frankly it's not strong enough to cover my own stink. I have been shitting in the woods for days with nothing but leaves and pine needles to wipe my ass. Throw in sweat and dirt and I bet you my pants would stand up by themselves. I'm going to have to be hosed off before I get a shower."

Jim realized that a shower and hot food were about the only things he missed about civilization. Huh. What was there that he needed? He didn't want to fit in again, all the stuff he'd fled from would just drag him down again. He felt different now, hard, rough, changed in a way he couldn't quite articulate. But he was sure he couldn't live the life he'd had before.

Buck raised his head and cocked his ear. Far off they could hear engine noise. Jim looked over at Buck. "Well that was a dose of reality. So much for our little idyll up here. You take the first watch, okay? I'm done in. Wake me if anything comes up."

Buck looked over at Jim and it seemed like he nodded his acknowledgement.

"Every joint and muscle in my body is aching. I'm feeling everything we have done these past few days. I'm not sure what's been worse, the climbing and riding or the sleeping on the cold hard ground. I tell you, Buck, I'm feeling every bit of my sixty plus years. We're done for the day and I need to just get some rest." He smiled. "I think some scotch would help."

Jim dug the flask of scotch out of the saddlebag. It was a twelve year old single malt that he had packed himself. He unscrewed the top and took a swig. "Ah, this is the nectar of the gods. Here, Buck, have a sniff." He held the open flask up to Buck's nose. Buck sneezed and then drew back his upper lip showing all his teeth. "Okay, okay. It's an acquired taste."

Jim felt the bite of the scotch go all the way down to his stomach. The second swig started to warm him. After the fourth, he could feel his body relax. He knew he could sleep for a few hours. The scotch was doing its job.

The night was still and cold. Jim made a bed of pine needles and wrapped himself up in his duster and covered that with the tarp he had found. He looked over at Buck and closed his eyes.

Buck stood watch over his man. He was tired but too keyed up to sleep. There had been those loud noises again today and the smells of blood and fear. He had taken his man to this place, away from the noises and the bad smells. It was good here. There was food and water. His man no longer smelled of fear.

When Jim started snoring Buck moved closer. He rested but did not sleep. Watching, listening, smelling, he guarded the man. The horse sighed and, collapsing his legs underneath, lay down next to Jim.

They would need the rest, more than Jim could ever guess.

Chapter 72

Jack had built a fire near the reservoir. He was pleased to find a cell phone on one of the dead men. After thoroughly searching the bodies, he'd made Chet help him drag the bodies into the trees. Chet bitched and whined about the killing. Using the phone he had Chet call his father to confirm delivery of the money. Only one man was to come, the money would be checked, and then Chet would be freed.

When it was full dark Botts and Fritz drove back from their lookout posts. Fritz had found the body of his missing friend along the trail.

"He was just lying there, the back of his head bashed in. No bullet wounds. Jesus, it creeps me out. Jack, do you think it was that same guy?" Fritz looked nervously between Jack and Botts.

"Probably. Was the body cold?"

"Yeah, that was bad. Flies were buzzing around it, too."

"That means it happened this morning. Whoever did it is long gone."

"Cheer up," Botts chipped in. "You get his share of the money. You're going to be rich."

"Okay, but do I have to go back there in the morning?" Fritz was whining like a child.

Jack grabbed him by the shirt front. "You go out there tomorrow or I'll kill you myself."

They gathered around the fire. Botts cooked them hot dogs and baked beans, looted from the fishermen's gear. Sitting around the fire they passed around a bottle of Jim Beam also found with the fishing gear. Chet and Fritz drank deeply, Jack and Botts sparingly.

Fritz was quiet. He was scared. His three friends were dead and he didn't want anything more to do with this mission. It wasn't a mission, it was a death trip and he was trapped. Big Jack would kill him if he tried to leave. If he survived, he was gonna go back home, live with mom and dad. Maybe go to tech school, find a girl, whatever as long he wasn't here. He took a big slug of whiskey, felt it burn.

"Jack," Botts asked, "do you think we should have Dude follow the money up here? We're shorthanded, especially if Fritz and I go back to our posts. It'll just be you and Chet here if there's a problem."

"Yeah, good idea. I'll call him in a minute. Have him follow a half mile back, make sure nobody is tailing the money. He can help with the tradeoff. Chet, you get to ride out with the delivery guy."

Chet burped. "What about my share?"

"Don't worry. My word is good. We're all set for tomorrow. This is going to happen without a hitch. We'll be out of here free and clear. We'll meet in Billings next week." Except you'll be dead, you dumb shit.

"Yeah, okay." He stood. "I'm going to take a leak." And wandered off into the night.

Jack looked at Botts and rolled his eyes. He gestured toward where Chet had gone. "We'll wait until we have the money in hand and take the ATV from the guy who brings the money. Then we'll ride out with Horvath."

Thirty yards away Chet was whispering into a cell phone he'd hidden in his pants. "That's right, there'll be a lookout and a guy following."

Davey Hopkins greeted the riders when they rode into Triangle Park. As he led them over to his camp he filled Zeke and Bob in.

"I've scouted most of the trail up to Ant Hill. Found that body at that switchback. Dragged it off the trail and covered it with a tarp."

"You hear anything when you were up there?"

"I snuck up and got close to the crest of the slope. Heard a small engine, probably an ATV, pretty near."

"That would be that lookout Jim told me about. We can't just ride up to the top of the trail. We'd be easy targets."

"Zeke, there's enough cover for me to get real close to anyone watching the trail. I can come in from the side, he won't be looking that way."

Zeke looked out at the darkened meadow, silver now in the moonlight.

"Davey, can you shoot him if you get a clear target?"

Davey looked at the sheriff and nodded. "Yep."

They walked in silence. When they got near the camp Davey looked over at Bob. "Hey, I've got a surprise for you."

"What?"

"Come look at my picket line."

239

Bob dismounted and walked over.

He laughed out loud. There, on Davey's picket line, were seven horses, Rosie and Bob's six missing horses.

Chapter 73

Jim woke. Buck was asleep right next to him. He looked off to the east. The stars were dimming and as he lay watching they faded into the lightning sky.

Jim never got tired of this view from the mountains. His imagination was fueled by it. Sometimes he felt he could see Wisconsin a thousand miles to the east. Other times he thought he could see the curvature of the earth, giant ball that it was. In the mornings the colors dazzled in their pastels, many shades of brown, from tan to rust, of green from bright alfalfa and grass to deep sage, red and dun earth, and blue water. Sometimes polka dotted by the moving shadows of small clouds. And at the far horizon all blending into the light blue and gray of the sky.

If he was lucky he could catch the sun slowly sneaking up the horizon and then become a huge, glowing, orange meatball. He thought of all of the people going about their everyday lives while he looked down upon them. Made him feel like a god.

Jim had a beer and some biscuits and watched the sun rise over the plains. Earth's star seemed to hesitate as it inched over the horizon. Was it reluctant to start this day? Then suddenly it was full up and the plains below changed from gray shadow to all the mixture of color. He fed Buck some cubes.

After a bit, he saddled Buck and took him down to the lake for a drink. Gem Lake was as flat as a mirror. Mist rose from the dark water, thin gray tendrils snaking up to form a layer of gauze a few feet above the surface. He looked off to the mountains in the west. Heavy clouds were boiling over the peaks, a deep bruised purple that seemed to absorb light and promise violence. As he watched, the clouds engulfed the mountains, great, fuzzy globules writhing and billowing in the distance. It seemed as though the clouds were alive and hungry, trying to devour the mountains. Jim felt a tingle in his spine, his reptile brain was stirring.

"Oh boy, Buck, those clouds look nasty. The sooner we get out of here the better, far away from those clouds and from the killers. Let's say we get a head start towards the trail so we're ready to go when things happen."

Buck nickered his agreement and they set off into the woods angling south and east. The sun from the east found gaps in the tree canopy, dappling the ground. The day was warming early. The deep green of the pine trees seemed to absorb the light and give back warmth. The needles on the ground crunched under Buck's hooves, millions of brown and orange needles complaining of the disruption of their repose.

Jim and Buck continued through the woods. They took a circuitous route around boulders and bramble patches, taking their time. He had no idea where the remaining killers were. Jim was edgy, he sure didn't want to meet the guy who had executed those poor fishermen. He decided to avoid the trail as long as he could. He kept scanning all around and let the horse pick his way. He checked his watch, only 9:00. Sheesh. According to Einstein clocks should run faster at this altitude.

They went on for an hour or so. There was a faint whiff of pine resin in the air. It was dry, not a hint of dew on the grass. Bob had said this was the fifth year of drought. This route was taking considerably longer than he had expected. He halted Buck.

It was quiet and still all around them. The forest seemed to be holding its breath. Then Jim heard the rumble of thunder, not that far away.

Chapter 74

Two trucks pulled into the trailhead parking lot, West Slope Drilling logos on the doors. A man got out of each truck and, without exchanging a word, unloaded an ATV from the back of one truck. From the other truck they hauled a large, square case. They strapped this to the back of the ATV. One man waved and got in his truck and drove off. A very nervous Jerry Harmon, security guard for West Slope, checked his watch, got on the machine and started up the rough road that led into the mountains.

A few hundred yards up the road he passed a man sitting on another ATV. He had been told to expect that. Dude Horvath started his engine as Jerry went past. After a minute of watching for other vehicles, Horvath followed.

Half way to the reservoir a man waited in a clump of brush near the road. Dressed in full camouflage gear and armed with a scoped rifle, Chas Brand, chief of West Slope security, watched the road below with binoculars. When both machines had passed he stood and followed.

Thirty minutes later the ATVs passed Botts' lookout

post. When Horvath went past Botts stood and waved. Following along the edge of the road, Chas Brand saw Botts wave. He slipped into the trees and continued upwards.

Chapter 75

The young FBI agent took the call from the Rapid City field office. When he was done he went to Doris.

"We traced the ATVs. I need to find a business here in the county. Some place called the Four Wheel Speed Shop. There's no listing in the phone book."

"I don't know the place and all the deputies are out. Maybe Sally Carter can help you."

Zeke was camped at Triangle Park when a call came in from dispatch.

"Sheriff," it was Doris. "I thought I should let you know. Some of those ATVs were traced to a business here called the Four Wheel Speed Shop. The FBI agent who stayed down here is going over there now. I sent Sally with him."

"Oh brother. Doris, Oscar Savage owns that shop. He's got a big chip on his shoulder about federal agents. Remember that hassle with ATF over those modified guns?"

"Yes. Didn't he lose his son over in Iraq?"

"Yep." He paused. "Look, there's nothing I can do right now. Call Jerry up at Flat Top if there's trouble."

Chapter 76

There was another rumble. The sky had darkened from purple to black, the light under the trees took on a greenish-yellow hue. The air became still and damp. He pulled on his duster and snapped it up, tightened the belt on his chaps. There was a puff of wind and it started to rain, not a sprinkle, but an out and out downpour. The rain roared and pounded down through the trees. It was deafening. Jim could feel the rain pepper him even under his duster. Jim pulled his hat down and turned up the collar of his duster.

Within a couple of minutes, any part of Buck not covered by Jim and the duster was soaking wet. Jim could barely see beyond Buck's head in the gloom and rain. Jim halted Buck. Stupid to try to ride in this deluge. They hunkered down to wait for it to let up.

Without warning--Boom! and then another boom! in the next second. Lightning hit close by. And again and again. Jim looked around. Although he could see very little, he knew that there was no safe place for them to go. Boom! Boom! The ground shook with every strike, the noise so loud that they both flinched with every blast. The rain was blinding and it was so dark Jim could barely see. The blasts rocked them, took their breath away.

Buck was quivering, Jim could feel it through the saddle. He had to do something, if they didn't get hit they'd likely go crazy. Do what? To get away from the trees made them a target; to stay under the trees left them as potential collateral damage. He kept telling himself "don't panic, don't panic. Panic will kill us both."

Crack! Wham! The flash was almost blinding and left an after image burned into his eyes. The strike had hit a big pine tree fifteen yards to the right. It crashed down like a giant axe had whacked it ten feet up from the ground. The top forty feet just tipped over and crashed top first onto the forest floor. In the next flash, Jim saw that the severed trunk still rested against the stump. It formed a tent of pine branches.

That was their shelter. Jim guided Buck over to the steaming wreck. They rode right under where the severed top of the tree leaned against its ten foot stump. It wasn't a perfect shelter from the rain but it did keep the worst of the downpour off them.

Jim and Buck huddled there, heads down, the rain splashing all around them. Lightning was still striking close by. The booms were deafening, but they were too punchy to flinch anymore. Jim kept patting Buck's neck and blabbering words at him.

"Buck, I know you're scared. I'm scared too but we're safe here. Just listen to me. I'll keep talking. Focus on me, forget everything else. Let me tell you about the time I was in an earthquake. It was 1972, before your mother was born. I was in Managua, Nicaragua. The middle of the night. Boom – just like this thunder except there was no storm. The house shook. I had no idea what was happening. I got up, boom – another earthquake. Now I knew what was happening because everything in the house was shaking and jumping. Finally I stumbled out of the house. The third earthquake hit. I watched the ground move like waves on a lake. It was awesome and terrifying at the same time. There was no place to hide from it. But it didn't get me. And now I'm here with you and we're hiding under this wrecked tree because there's nowhere else to hide."

Then Jim started murmuring the lyrics of songs to Buck. He wanted to keep Buck's attention focused on his voice and to distract himself from the chaos all around them. He sang, very off key, Gordon Lightfoot's Edmund Fitzgerald. Then Forty Thousand Headmen from Traffic and Me and My Uncle from The Grateful Dead. This seemed to be working. Both man and horse focused on the songs. Jim launched into a rendition of Jerry Jeff Walker's Up Against the Wall Red Neck Mother.

The smell of ozone was so strong it was intoxicating. It overpowered the pine scent and the smell of rain and wet horse, even the rank char from their shelter. He felt as if he were inside the electric grid for the universe.

Even with his hat and duster, Jim was getting soaked. The rain found gaps in his gear. Water was running down his neck. Soon his duster was saturated and moisture was seeping into his clothes where the duster was snug. Buck was totally soaked even under his mane. They were both getting chilled but there was nothing to be done. Just endure.

"Roland was a warrior from the land of the midnight sun, with a Thompson gun for hire..." He sang until he was hoarse.

"Buck, we haven't lived through this ordeal, guns and killing and hiding and all, just to get done in by some damn storm. We're going to get through this. We're going to get back down to town. Then we're going eat and sleep all we want. We'll tell everyone about this and they won't believe us. But you and I will know. And if we ever get bored, we'll think back on this and say bored is good."

Buck focused all his attention on his man's voice. Like a lifeline to a drowning man he clung to it. There was danger all around, beyond anything he'd ever experienced. He had heard thunder before and smelled lightning, but he had always been safely in a barn. Now he felt each blast on his skin and in his bones. Only his man's voice kept him from panic and flight. He must stay with his man, his man would protect him.

They stayed like that for what seemed like ages. Man and horse together with the world raging all around them.

Jim thought no profound thoughts nor said any prayers. He was awed by the power of nature unmitigated by any artificial structure. He was grateful to have Buck's loyal companionship in this maelstrom and was content to know that he would share Buck's fate.

And then it stopped. As suddenly as it started, the storm moved off. The thunder was just a distant rumble. The sun came out. Jim and Buck stirred. They had survived.

They were soaked through to the skin and cold. Buck turned his head and looked at Jim.

"Yeah, enough of this. Let's move out and get off this mountain and get to town."

With that they started off again weaving their way through the now dripping trees.

Chapter 77

Jerry Harmon had just got to the reservoir when the storm hit. He'd been so intent on his mission and deafened by the engine noise that the downpour took him completely by surprise. The rain was like a wall of water and forced him to stop. Surprise turned to terror when jagged forks of lightning plunged into the open water with cracks of thunder so loud he could feel the sound waves. He jumped off the machine and crouched in a ditch next to the road.

Coming up behind, Dude Horvath drove through the rain until he got to the reservoir. When he saw the other ATV through the sheets of rain he dismounted. Over the din of the storm he heard Jack shout his name. He crept into the trees opposite the water and watched the first machine and its cargo as best he could, the flashes of lightning illuminating it every few seconds. He prayed that the lightning wouldn't strike the ransom.

Botts was hunkered down at his lookout post. He was blinded by the rain and could hear nothing over the roar of the rain and the crashes and booms of thunder. Visibility was a mere few feet in the trees and brush. Fuck, when would this let up? He put his hand above his eyes and squinted at the road. Nobody could come up in this. Between lightning strikes he thought he heard a voice. Then he heard it again.

"Hello, Botts."

He turned and saw a hooded figure a couple of feet behind him. As he reached for the pistol under his jacket the bullet entered his forehead. He never heard the report of the gun.

Chapter 78

Jack, Horvath, and Chet staggered out from the trees. Clothes dripping wet and hair plastered down, they looked around the clearing next to the reservoir. Bright sunlight shimmered on the puddles of water, rainwater already steaming and evaporating. The air smelled fresh and clean. Across from them the water in the reservoir was calm and sparkled and beyond the granite peaks stood in silent indifference.

Horvath looked up at the sky and shook his head. "Holy fuck, where did that mother of a frog choker come from?"

"I thought we were goners. Thank god the ransom got here when it did." Chet was babbling. "Did you see that lightning hit the water?"

Big Jack snorted. "Come on, ladies, let's check the money."

As they approached the ATV with the big case Jerry Hanson stood up in the ditch. His clothes were covered in mud. Eyes glazed and mouth agape, he looked bewildered. When he focused on the three figures approaching him he spoke.

"Mr. Stevens, are you okay?"

Chet just waved in response.

As Jack got closer Jerry stuttered, "JJJack. You're Big Jack. What are you doing here? Chief Brand didn't say anything about you being here."

Jack smiled. "Hi, Jerry. Where's Chas?"

"I don't know. He just told me to drive up here and get Mr. Stevens." He looked around. "Supposed to deliver the ransom to the kidnappers."

"Change of plans, Jerry." Jack walked right up to him, pulled his pistol from his belt, and put the gun to Jerry's ear. "Where's Chas?" He cocked the hammer.

Jerry shivered. Shaking his head he mumbled, "I don't know. I'm just doing what I was told."

"Last chance, Jerry," Jack said with a smile, his eyes gleaming. Jerry just stood there shaking. He closed his eyes. With a sob he pissed his pants. Jack fired. Blood and gore spewed from the other side of Jerry's head and he fell backwards into the ditch.

"Jesus, Jack, why?" Chet bent over and vomited.

Jack yanked him upright. "The fucking money is here you chicken shit. Do you want it or not?"

Chet nodded and wiped his mouth on his sleeve and followed Jack to the ATV.

The three men opened the case and each grabbed a bundle of money. "Dude, let's get this into the packs."

Horvath grinned. "Man, this is sweet. Glad we have these machines, there's a lot to carry."

"Four hundred eighty bills to the pound. I did my research."

They quickly stuffed the bundles of money into the frame packs Horvath had brought. While Jack and Horvath were occupied Chet glanced at the body of the security man then looked off down the road. He reached into a pants pocket and gripped his cell phone, a worried expression on his face.

Just as they were finishing Horvath jerked forward as the others heard the gunshot. He fell forward and flopped to the ground next to the machine. He landed face first in the mud and twitched, blood oozing from a hole in his back. Before the body even hit the ground, Jack grabbed one of the packs and ran for the trees. The second shot would have hit Chet if he hadn't reached for the other bag. Instead the bullet kicked up mud at his feet.

Chet stood and yelled, "Chas, it's me, Chet."

The next shot banged into the ATV behind him. Chet hesitated only a moment then ran after Jack, all thought of the money forgotten.

Chas Brand stepped out of the woods and looked around. He fired a couple of rounds in the direction Jack and Chet had fled. He chuckled and ran over to the other pack. Picking it up he turned and pulled out the gas line on that machine. Then he disabled Horvath's ATV and trotted down the road where he'd left Botts' ATV.

Chapter 79

The Four Wheel Speed Shop had seen better days. The cinder block structure needed paint and sat on a potholed gravel lot off a frontage road by the interstate eight miles south of town. Strewn about the lot were several vehicles in various states of disrepair including a Mack semi-tractor, a Case end loader, an army surplus jeep, and a Dodge pickup jacked high on outsized tires.

The FBI agent, Bill Curran, with Sally Carter riding along, pulled to a stop in front of the building and parked next to two three wheeled ATVs. They went up the cement steps and entered the shop.

Oscar Savage stood behind a counter covered with shop manuals, phone books, and unopened mail. Savage's five six frame was topped with stringy gray hair which appeared to not have seen a comb or shampoo in quite some time. Gray stubble covered his weathered face and his faded and grease stained coveralls were open to his waist and revealed a food spotted t- shirt. He wiped grease off his gnarled hands with a shop rag.

His initial smile disappeared when the federal agent held up his credentials.

"Special Agent Curran, FBI. Are you the owner of this business?"

"Mister Federal Agent you can shove that ID where the sun don't shine. Get out of my shop. I'm closed and you're trespassing."

"Sir, we're investigating a . . ."

"I don't care if you're investigating the Queen of England. Get out." He picked up an ax handle from behind the counter.

The agent stiffened and unbuttoned his jacket. He started to reach for the gun on his belt.

Sally was watching the men. She knew she had to defuse this and fast. She stepped forward. Sally looked like a child on vacation with her stick limbs poking out of pink shorts and aqua t-shirt emblazoned with the face of Snow White.

She stood between the two men, arms spread.

"Whoa. Mr. Savage, I'm Sally Carter. Remember me?"

Savage shifted his gaze, looked hard at Sally.

"Mr. Savage, you know me. My big brother and your son were in high school together."

Savage's face softened. "Jeff played football with my Ron. They both went to Eye Rack."

"Yes, sir. And neither one came back."

Sally leaned on the counter and looked up at Oscar Savage. "Mr. Savage, I'm working for Sheriff Thomasen."

Savage grunted. "Zeke's a good old boy. What's he doing with the god durned FBI?"

"Please, Mr. Savage, forget the FBI. Talk to me."

"I can't forget the damn federals. They harassed me about my guns, took them, and they, they. . ." he grimaced. "They sent my boy home in a pine box."

"I'm sorry, Mr. Savage. I miss Jeff terribly, too. But please, will you talk with me?"

Oscar Savage sighed. "Okay, I'll talk to you, Sally. What do you want? If it's about the protest at Flat Top, I wasn't there."

"It's not that. There's been a murder and kidnapping. The kidnappers drove six ATVs. Four of them trace back to your shop. I, we need your help. I've got the serial numbers right here."

"Oh, hell, I don't need them numbers. I thought it was weird, one guy buying six machines. I had to bring two down from Nathan's in Sheridan. Guy paid me cash. Said he'd have his men come by to pick them up."

"Did he give you a name?"

Savage rubbed the stubble on his chin. "Nope."

Sally's shoulders sagged. She looked over at the agent and back at Savage. "Anything you remember about him, anything at all?"

"He was a nervous fella, that's for sure." He paused. "Let me think. Yeah, I remember. His wife came in and yapped at him. Called him . . ."

Agent Curran had been quiet but interrupted. "He had a wife with him?"

"That's right, Mister Federal Agent. Now shut up." Savage closed his eyes. "The wife came in. She said a name." He paused and scratched under his arm. "'The kids want to eat, hurry up.' Guy didn't look too happy about it." He bit a knuckle. "I just can't remember the name she used."

Sally shrugged. "Thanks, Mr. Savage. That helps. If you think of the name will you call me at the Sheriff Office?"

"Yep, Honey, I will."

Chapter 80

Jim and Buck were happy to be moving. It would warm them up. When they got out from under the trees, the mountain sunshine would dry them quickly in the arid air. Life was good. They'd be in town tonight.

They heard gunfire. Jim looked at his watch. It was well after ten. "Buck, let's get going. Time to make our exit."

They bulled their way through branches and brush heading straight for the trail. In a few minutes they burst through the last tangle of branches and thorns and onto the trail. The sunlight had dimmed. Jim stopped Buck and looked around. There was no sign of anyone, killers or cops. He was about to turn Buck toward Ant Hill when he heard engine noise from that direction.

It was that lookout heading back to the reservoir. Had to be. Bastard.

He thought about hiding until the man passed. Then their route would be clear. Just let him go by. But they'd killed Dave and executed those poor fucking fishermen. Taken their lives. Could have tied them up. These fuckers enjoyed killing. They came to this beautiful place and fouled it in the worst way. Let him go by? No fucking way.

Jim jumped down and dug the coil of rope from the saddle bags. "Buck, we're going to bushwhack this SOB." He ran across the trail and tied one end of the rope to a thick pine tree at about waist height. Then he ran back to Buck and tied the other end to the saddle horn. The rope had enough slack so that it was flat on the trail, impossible to see from a speeding ATV.

Jim mounted up. "Buck, you know what we're going to do, don't you? Wait for my signal." The horse looked at him and snorted. "God damn, I'm gonna get this bastard."

They waited in the trees at the edge of the trail. The horse and rider calm, muscles loose and ready.

In less than a minute the ATV came racing down the trail. Jim gave the signal when the machine got within thirty feet. He pulled back on the reins and pushed his feet forward in the stirrups. Buck backed up quickly and the rope rose just as the machine came even with them.

It all happened in what seemed to be a split second. The rope caught the man right in the throat. The rope twanged with the impact and Jim felt the saddle jerk. At the speed he was going, Jim knew the man would be just about decapitated. The rope lifted the driver off the seat and his body flew off the back of the machine. The body seemed to hang in the air for a second or two then landed flat on the trail. The machine veered off the trail and crashed into the trees with a huge crunch. The engine quit.

Stunned, Jim and Buck were stock still in the sudden silence. Then Jim blew out a "whew," and took the rope off the saddle horn and let it drop to the ground as if it were poison. He rode Buck out onto the trail.

Jim knew the man was dead but took a look anyway.

The body was flat on its back spread eagled. The head, while still somewhat attached, was in a growing pool of blood with blood still pumping from the severed arteries in the neck.

Buck shied away from the blood. Jim had to grit his teeth and swallow down the rising bile. He shuddered. "Buck, that was too easy." He took a deep breath and closed his eyes, blew out a breath. "Jesus." Jim shivered. He bent forward, put his arms around Buck's neck, and pressed his face to the horse's mane.

Buck turned his head, bumped Jim's foot with his nose, and snorted.

"Yeah, okay, I'll save it for later. Let's get out of this mess."

Chapter 81

They were leading the horses up the last quarter mile of the trail. Soaking wet after the storm, they squished their way up slope.

"Damn, Bob, nobody counted on that gully washer this morning. I hope it didn't delay the ransom."

"Don't know about that, but from all the thunder we heard down below they must have been ducking lightning the whole time."

Zeke grunted his agreement.

They halted when they were just below the crest to wait for Davey Hopkins who'd gone ahead to scout for the lookout.

"Zeke, are we going to wait for the FBI or are we going to go look for Jim?"

"He's been left on his own long enough. To hell with the FBI, we're going to find him."

Davey came bounding back a few minutes later.

"Sheriff, the guy is gone. I found the four wheeler tracks and I heard its engine. He was heading toward the reservoir." The deputy caught his breath. "There's a big problem. You'd better see for yourself. You won't believe it."

They mounted up and rode to the crest. They halted and took in the panorama.

From the high ground they saw a massive cloud of smoke covering the northern horizon. As they watched the smoke billowed higher and a red glow was visible underneath. Bob and Zeke groaned.

"Holy shit! It's coming this way and the wind's moving it pretty good."

"Bob, the fire's going to take the whole plateau. There's not much time. We've got to leave."

The horses were starting to prance as the scent of smoke hit them.

"Zeke, what about Jim? He's up here somewhere. We've got to get him out of here."

"Bob, I know it. But we can't stay up here. We've got to head back. Now." Zeke turned to his deputies and waved them off. "Come on, Bob. We're no help to anybody if we get burned up."

Bob hung his head. "He's a goner, isn't he?"

"He'd need a miracle." Zeke sighed. "Let's go."

Bob took a last look then turned his horse and followed the sheriff.

Chapter 82

They had gone only a quarter mile toward Ant Hill when they came upon the body of the man they had killed two days before. Flies were swarming around and on it. Jim tried not to look, but he could smell it. The corpse stank of rot and excrement. They gave it a wide berth, Buck muttering as they passed. The buzzing of the flies seemed angry and accusative to Jim. What had once been a person was now just rotting meat. He had turned the man into this.

And then there was a new smell.

Smoke! That was smoke blowing toward them through the tree tops. Somehow Jim knew it wasn't from a camp fire. "Buck, I don't like this. I hope I'm wrong."

They started walking toward Ant Hill. The smell of smoke grew stronger. It seemed to be following them. Jim looked up. The sky was darkening, the sun thickly filtered by smoke. The smell was stronger now. Buck sneezed. It stung Jim's nose and made his eyes water.

Jim stopped Buck and looked around. The ancient part of his brain was screaming "danger, flee". He stood in the stirrups. The thickest smoke was due north and billowing up into black roiling clouds. The smoke was driven by a strong wind from the northwest. He could hear a roar in the distance. It all meant only one thing. "Holy shit!"

Jim shook his head. After all that rain, how could there be a fire? Then he remembered that this was the fifth year of drought in the Big Horns. The trees were tinder dry. It would take a week of steady rain to alter that. The lightning strikes had set off this fire and the wind was doing the rest. It was really happening. Talk about out of the frying pan. Stop it. Think, what to do?

If they went south and east toward Ant Hill, the fire would be behind them. It would be a race. How far would the fire run? Would it jump the treetops? It would be impossible to race down the Ant Hill trail. It was a slow, switchback descent. If the wind didn't change, they would be overtaken on their way down.

There was only one other way to go. Just thinking about it made Jim clench his teeth. They could race across the front of the fire and get beyond its path. If the fire caught them, they'd be roasted alive. Two choices. He had to decide now or it wouldn't matter. If the wind didn't shift, the Ant Hill trail was a death trap. Couldn't count on that. He'd rather trust Buck's speed. Okay, the other way. Do it.

"Buck, there's only one thing to do. You've got to trust me. We're going to go back towards the fire – run to the reservoir – it's our only hope. You've got to fly." And if I'm wrong, we're dead.

Jim turned Buck and kicked him to a gallop. Buck blasted up to full speed, his training overcoming any fear he had of the smoke and fire. They raced along the trail. Within a minute the smoke got thicker, visibility got worse and worse. Jim looked back over his shoulder. He could see flames on both sides of the trail. They'd left just in time. He leaned forward half crouched over Buck's neck, his butt almost out of the saddle, his hand with the reins stretched forward. Being still wet from the storm gave them some protection from the heat being blown at them from the oncoming blaze, but the air was so hot that it hurt to breathe.

The fire was roaring toward them, a sucking, whooshing, consuming roar. Jim heard another noise and looked back again. The trail had disappeared. Fifty yards behind was a solid wall of flame. Bright orange tentacles twisted and coiled.

Suddenly they were in a thick patch of smoke. Jim could barely see the trail ahead. He tried not to breathe. He worried that the smoke wouldn't do Buck any good either. Luckily, the thickest smoke was higher than Buck's head. In his gallop, Buck had his head down and his back rounded. His nose was only a couple of feet off the ground. He had been trained to run this way. The training now gave this unexpected dividend.

Buck was a running machine. The powerful muscles in his quarter horse rear end pumping and pumping, hind feet coming under him then propelling them forward, his hooves pounding and pounding. He willingly raced through the smoke and fire. It was flight, instinct for him. His man encouraged his effort even when the heat intensified and he could see flames. He ran with his man. His man knew where to go.

Jim focused straight ahead. He could feel the heat, saw fire in the corner of his eye. He was afraid to look directly at the fire, felt that if he did the fire would engulf them. It was all up to Buck. Buck was flying, everything was a blur except

Buck. He had never ridden this fast. Buck was all muscle in motion. He clung with his knees and with his hands in Buck's mane, crouched like a jockey. If Buck stumbled, they would both be goners.

Jim could feel Buck starting to tire, his gait getting rough. Jim yelled in Buck's ears, "come on, Buck. You've got the juice."

Buck snorted and regained his rhythm.

Jim stared ahead, willing the reservoir to appear. His whole right side was stinging hot, soon his clothes would ignite. Boom! A tree exploded and they were showered with sparks. He brushed a glowing bit off Buck's neck.

Finally the trail widened and they were at the approach to the reservoir. As they went past the junction, Jim took a quick look around. Saw objects but was so intent on escape he couldn't put names on them. Buck slowed to a trot as they went down slope to the overflow stream next to the dam. They got into the stream. Jim guided Buck out toward the open water of the reservoir. When the water was up to Buck's belly they stopped and turned to look behind.

It was impossible to see the trail they had just left. The nearest part was obscured by smoke. Beyond that was a wall of fire blazing above the treetops and roaring toward Ant Hill. Tongues of yellow and orange and red clawing at the sky, billows of sparks and ashes driven by the heat and the wind, the fire seemed a living thing devouring the forest. The noise was incredible – a roaring as loud as jet planes taking off. Every few seconds there was a crackling boom as trees were literally exploding from the heat of the fire.

They could feel some of the heat from the fire, but they were safe. The nearest trees were almost a hundred yards away. The fire was angling away from them. Buck was breathing hard, nostrils flared. He shook himself and lowered his head and drank.

"Buck, we did it. You did it." Jim leaned forward and hugged the horse's neck. "We're safe here. We can wait out the fire. If it gets too hot, I'll splash water on us. If the wind shifts we could get a lot of smoke, but the fire won't get us."

Buck turned his head and looked at Jim. His eyes showed the extreme strain he had just been through and seemed to say "enough, please, enough."

Jim reached down and stroked his neck. "Me too, Buck, me too."

Chapter 83

Moving quietly through the greenish light, Jack was a hundred yards into the trees when he heard crashing and thrashing behind him. He lowered the heavy pack to the ground and squatted behind a pine tree. He raised his pistol.

Chet burst through a tangle of brush and tripped over the pack. He fell head first, catching himself with his hands. He quickly got up on his hands and knees. Turning his head, he looked directly into the bore of Jack's pistol.

Panting, he choked out, "no, please, don't shoot me. I can explain."

"You little fuck. You double crossed me. You had Chas follow the ransom so he could kill me and you could take all the money. You'd planned this from the gitgo." And that rat bastard Chas killed Dude and probably Botts, too.

"No, no. I just wanted to make sure you didn't take my share. Chas was my insurance," Chet whimpered.

"Bullshit. But the joke's on you. He was in this for himself and tried to kill you. With you dead he could hide the money and tell your old man that I'd already killed you or he could just disappear with the money. Either way, he was going to fuck you over."

"What are we going to do? He's coming after us."

"Cut the 'we' shit, you stinking weasel. I'm going to hike in and find a good spot for an ambush. Chas will either come after me or take half the money and leave. You're fucked either way." If Chas doesn't come now I will hunt him down and kill him like a dog. The fucker killed my guys, the last men from my unit.

Chet looked back toward the reservoir. "Please, I don't want to die," he whined.

Jack ignored him and trudged deeper into the forest. Chet stumbled after him. A quarter mile further he stopped to rest. He lay prone behind a log. Chet came up and flopped down next to him.

Jack sniffed. Sneezed. Sat up.

Smoke! What was this now? The first tendrils of smoke quickly became an acrid fog. Then there was the noise, a roaring and crackling deeper in the forest, getting closer.

"Sweet Baby Jesus! The woods are on fire. It's a forest fire. Fuck!"

He stood up and hefted the pack onto his back. The smoke was drifting through the trees and getting so thick Jack could barely see. His eyes were tearing up and his throat was raw. He and Chet were coughing and hacking.

They stumbled and staggered through the smoke. Visibility was so bad that they often tripped over rocks and logs and got tangled in brush, forcing them to scramble on hands and knees. The noise of the fire was an ever-present roar. The roar kept them moving. The fire was an unseen beast chasing them. They couldn't tell how close the inferno was and not even Jack was brave enough to stop and look back.

The roar got louder. There were explosions. They could feel the heat now. Chet tripped over a log and fell. As he ran Jack heard Chet's screams over the roar of the fire, then the screams stopped. Eyes burning, struggling for air, he burst out of the trees and onto the ATV road. Smoke was billowing over the road and the heat was as intense as a blast furnace. Jack ran across the road bent under the heavy pack.

Several hundred feet below, down a slope of boulders, was a small lake with a gravel shore. He was wheezing and coughing so much that Jack knew he had to get down there, to stay on the road was to die of the smoke if the fire didn't roast him first.

He struggled to climb down the boulder field under the weight of the pack. Still hacking and half blind, he tried to hurry. The moss and lichen on the rocks were slippery from the earlier storm. Hopping from boulder to boulder while trying to balance the load on his back, Jack fell onto his hands and elbows several times. Near the bottom Jack lost his footing, twisted his ankle, and screamed, then fell and cracked his head on a boulder. Bundles of money spilled from the pack and split apart, hundred dollar bills fluttered and landed in the rocks and onto the water.

Limping, coughing, gagging he dragged himself to the shore of the lake. He collapsed next to the water. Jack realized he was in no condition to go any further. His lungs were on fire, wheezing and hacking. White hot pain in his ankle, head throbbing, dizzy, Jack retched until he lost consciousness.

Chapter 84

Jim might have enjoyed the spectacle of the raging fire – a rare opportunity to watch a forest fire up close yet safely – were it not for his concern about Buck. Horses fear fire and, although he was a safe distance from it, Buck was muttering and swinging his head from side to side. Also, Jim didn't think Buck was happy standing belly deep in cold water. He was a most sensible horse and willingly followed Jim's lead, but this was close to overload.

Jim worried about the sheriff and Bob. They were coming up the trail to Ant Hill. That put them in the direct path of the fire. Had they fled quickly enough? Where had they gone? Had they raced the fire down the mountain? Had they found a safe place to wait it out? Bob was a savvy woodsman, if anyone could find an escape it would be Bob.

And then what about the kidnappers and Chet and the ransom? When he and Buck raced up to the reservoir he'd seen two ATVs in the clearing and thought he'd glimpsed a body. Had the others left before the fire? Where was that bald bastard? Chet? Were they now roasty-toasties? Had they gone far enough north to be beyond where the fire had started?

Speculation was useless. Time to do something to ease

his horse's anxiety. Jim had Buck walk back up the overflow stream a little way to where they could climb up onto the dam itself. It was made of gravel, a horse could walk on it easily. The dam was far enough away from the trees to be safe. If things got too hot, they could always get back into the water.

They climbed onto the dam and walked toward the far side. The trees to the west were not on fire and would probably stay that way unless the wind shifted. When they got to the far end of the dam, Jim turned Buck around. Jim looked about. The fire kept marching to the southeast toward Ant Hill, smoke filling the sky, black with an under glow of red and orange. Closer by, the remains of the forest smoldered. To the west, all was quiet, the tall peaks watching impassively, their rock faces immune. One hundred feet below the dam was Flat Iron Lake, its still waters reflecting the sun. And there was something along the shore lying in the rocks. A body?

Jim took out his binoculars. Yes, it was a human body down there. Pieces of paper were fluttering about. There was no movement or other sign of life. Smoke drifted across the little lake, the water still and smooth as a mirror.

Was it dead or alive? No way to tell from up on the dam and no way to get to him without going into the fire zone.

To the north everything was black, smoke drifting. He had no idea if it was safe for them to head down the road. So Jim and Buck waited on the dam.

Waiting was okay for now. They would need to leave this place, couldn't stay indefinitely. He and Buck were out of food and exhausted. For the moment he could postpone the return to civilization. Hot food and a hot shower would be nice but he wasn't ready to be with people.

Huh.

He was so used to having Buck as his sole companion that the idea of being around people seemed somehow alien. Wasn't sure he could make polite conversation any more.

Buck interrupted his funk with a nicker.

"Okay, Bud, I'd best see to you."

Jim unsaddled Buck and groomed him as best he could. He had a small brush in his saddle bags and he found a comb in his pocket. As he groomed, he talked.

"Well, this isn't much in the way of equipment but we're in no hurry. I see you haven't got any sores under the saddle pad despite all the wet. You've got a bunch of twigs in your mane and tail. Don't know how much I can get out with this comb."

This mundane routine relaxed them both. After a few minutes, Buck gave a great sigh and closed his eyes. Jim felt the tension leave his own body replaced by fatigue. After about a half hour he sat down near Buck and leaned against a small boulder. The sun had dried any moisture that the fire hadn't. He napped.

When his man sat down, Buck opened his eyes. Although relaxed, he was still alert to his surroundings. He was, after all, a prey animal and had certainly seen enough danger this day to send most horses into panicked flight.

The sun felt good on his back. He found a few blades of grass to nibble on. The wind had mellowed to a mild breeze but it still bore the scent of smoke. He knew that he was safe from the fire. The water of the reservoir interested him, the sunlight sparkling on the ripples. He had no urge to move. He would stay put and watch over his man.

Chapter 85

Attorney General Albert Basset, III, stood on the front steps of the Sheriff Department building and gazed out at the crowd. He was in his element. He patted his hair, puffed up his five six frame, and unbuttoned his suit. He waited for the camera crews to set up and the print reporters to quiet their conversations.

Doris Wilburn looked out her window. She knew the politician had betrayed her sheriff. Now he was going to claim credit for the efforts that he had done his best to hinder. As the Attorney General prepared to address the media Doris turned from the window, put her glasses on her nose, and picked up her telephone.

When the TV crews were ready Basset cleared his throat. He smiled for the cameras. He was going to nail down some votes.

"The people of Wyoming are proud of the efforts of our law enforcement personnel. Their bravery and persistence in dealing with this crisis are to be commended. Our plans are about to result in the capture of these dangerous criminals and the rescue of an innocent victim."

When Basset paused to catch his breath, Alf Jacobson,

editor, publisher, and reporter for the Bison Banner shouted a question.

"Mr. Attorney General, is it true that Sheriff Thomasen requested assistance from the State Patrol and that you refused to send help? That you left our Sheriff Department to deal with this kidnapping and the protest at Flat Top without any support from your office?"

Doris, again looking out her window, had a satisfied grin on her face as the Attorney General sputtered and deflated.

Chapter 86

Toward dusk they heard the sound of a helicopter approaching from the west. Jim waved and did a kind of jumping jack dance. The helicopter hovered over the reservoir, the wash from the rotors buffeting them. It looked like a small one, a two seater. A voice came over a loud speaker. "Are you with the Sheriff's party? Have you seen the others?"

There was no point in yelling, so Jim pointed down toward Flat Iron Lake. The voice continued, "You can get out on the road to the north. The fire is well past. We have help coming up from the trailhead."

Jim gave a two thumbs up signal and waved again toward Flat Iron. The copter apparently got the message as it moved off in that direction and then slowly dropped down to where the prone figure lay.

Jim saddled Buck and mounted. "Come on old friend, they say we can get out of here. Let's go." And they walked back across the dam and then over to the ATV road. Jim saw two bodies. Neither one was the bald guy nor Chet.

Their ride out was eerie and surreal. On the east side of the road were blackened, smoking trees and brush. Most trees stood like telephone poles, black with all branches and boughs burnt clean off. A forest of black poles littered with the fallen which lay every which way. Embers glowed in the shadows. Smoke and stink made it hard to breathe. The heat from the burn was still so intense that it forced them to keep to the far edge of the road. To Jim it was as if hell had paid a visit to the Big Horns, taking the forest and leaving char, stink, and heat. Jim was tempted to ask Buck to go faster but knew that the horse was close to exhaustion.

By the time it was full dark, they were beyond the fire zone. Jim got down and led Buck. They plodded along on the gentle down slope, their way lit by the stars. After another mile or so, they heard voices up ahead. In a few minutes, they saw lights. Jim and Buck stopped and waited, happy to stop moving.

Soon they were surrounded by people in uniform, led by a squad of cops in riot gear. Their leader stopped Jim and asked for identification. When he checked Jim's drivers' license he shook Jim's hand. Jim silently thanked the sheriff.

"Sir, have you seen anyone else since the fire?"

"There were two bodies near the reservoir and a body below the dam. No one I recognized."

"Any sign of Mr. Stevens?"

"No."

"Okay, thanks." And the cops marched on.

Then they were approached by paramedics. Jim waved them off. "We need food and water. We need to rest," he croaked.

Someone gave him a bottle of water. Jim poured it into his hat and gave it to Buck.

Escorted by rescue workers, Jim and Buck finished the

trek to the trailhead. By the time they got there Jim was staggering and leaning on his horse who wasn't doing much better. The scene there was chaotic, with ambulances, fire trucks, and squad cars all jumbled about. There were many people in uniform milling under portable lights and around several large tents.

After their sojourn in the mountains, they found the lights and noise and all the people moving about to be disorienting. They just wanted quiet and rest. A community of two, they were not ready to rejoin civilization.

Jim led Buck to a small paddock, found him a bucket of water and some flakes of hay. He took off the saddle and bridle. A woman in medical scrubs came over and handed Jim a mug of coffee and a sandwich. Jim sat by the paddock fence to eat.

"Sir, we need to check you over. Would you please come with me?"

"No, ma'am." He was having trouble talking. "I'm just exhausted. What you gave me here will be just fine. I just need some rest. Has anyone heard from Bob Lundsten or the sheriff?"

"I wouldn't know. I'll ask around. We can get you a ride into town and your horse will be fine here until morning."

"Sorry, but no way am I leaving Buck here. We both go or neither of us goes. We've had quite a time of it up there, just the two of us." So right now just let us be.

"Okay, suit yourself," she huffed, not trying to conceal her irritation. "We have food and drinks at the tent over there. We're expecting the rescue chopper any minute so I'll be going."

Jim finished eating and found a soft spot in the grass

next to the paddock away from the lights. He lay down and bundled up once again in his duster. It was over. They had finally made it down. Buck's rhythmic chewing and munching on hay soothed him. He drifted in and out of sleep. He heard the noise of the helicopter landing, then dropped off again.

Chapter 87

He woke. He was lying on his back. Through closed eyes, he could sense bright light. There was something over his nose and mouth. He tried to move his hands and legs – movement, but not much. He was restrained somehow, couldn't move his arms. Cautiously, Jack opened his eyes to slits. Instruments, monitors. He was in some kind of hospital or clinic. He heard voices and closed his eyes and listened.

"He's suffering from smoke inhalation, a concussion, and a badly sprained ankle. I expect him to be unconscious for hours. We're giving him oxygen and we've put a walking boot on his ankle. We should be able to transfer him in the morning, get him out of this tent and into the hospital in town."

"Doctor, did you find any identification on him? We have him for murder and kidnapping. We've found two bodies near where we found him. The man he kidnapped is still missing. Let me know as soon as he's conscious. We need to know where his hostage is and the rest of his accomplices."

"We found no I.D. He's in his late thirties or early forties, good health, has taken care of himself. No distinguishing marks or tattoos."

"Okay. I'm going to post a guard right outside. Let us know when he comes around."

Jack made no outward sign that he was conscious. He remembered a helicopter touching down by the lake and black clad troopers swarming and being handcuffed. Captured and the money gone. Shit, shit, shit, he'd failed.

But he wasn't in jail, not yet. Apparently he was in some kind of first aid tent. He would find a chance for escape. The mission had failed but he was not going to be caged. He would find a way. And then he'd hunt down Chas Brand.

———————

Someone came into the room. The rustle of clothes, scent of perfume. A woman, probably a nurse. Whoever it was picked up his wrist, checking his pulse he guessed. How to get these restraints off? He needed a plan. Maybe if they thought he was dying they'd take them off to examine him. A heart attack? No. Convulsions or a stroke? Yes.

Jack started coughing and thrashing and gasping, his whole body tensed. He bounced his torso up and down. Let out a gurgling moan. A woman's voice, "guard, help me here." He kept thrashing, bouncing. "He's having a grand mal, hold his legs." He felt the restraints released. He bucked and thrashed wildly now, felt hands grab his legs, felt hands on his face.

He risked a peek. The nurse had a stethoscope to his chest. A man in uniform was bent over his legs holding them down. There was a holstered gun in his belt. Jack kicked and thrashed harder, arched his torso up and down. Make it hard to hold me, make them work, use all of their concentration.

Now. He jerked himself up to a sitting position and,

282

without pause, reached and grabbed the pistol, flicked off the safety. The guard lunged at him. He fired into the man's chest. The guard staggered backwards and fell. The woman screamed and moved toward the fallen guard.

He swung his legs out of bed and stood. He ripped off the mask from his face. He felt a little dizzy and wobbly but he could stand on the bad ankle with the boot on.

The nurse was bent over the guard. Jack grabbed her arm and yanked her upright. He put an arm around the woman's neck and jammed the gun in her back. "Nurse," he growled, "you're going to help me get out of here. Do exactly as I say and you will live. Try to escape and I will shoot. Understand?"

The nurse nodded, sobbing.

"Okay, we're going to walk out of this tent. You'll be my shield."

Chapter 88

The gunshot woke him. He shook himself and opened his eyes. Did he dream that?

Jim sat up in the knee high grass. He looked over towards the tents and lights. About a half a dozen cops were standing in front of the biggest tent. Between them and him, he saw a man standing and holding another person around the neck. The man's back was to Jim so he couldn't see who it was.

One of the cops stepped toward the man. He heard the report of a gunshot and the cop collapsed.

"Oh, Judas Priest. This is not happening."

The man was shouting at the cops, but Jim couldn't make out what he was saying. The man was backing up toward Jim using the other person as a shield.

The man was about twenty yards away. Jim pulled out his revolver. He didn't dare take a shot for fear of hitting the hostage. He crouched in the tall grass next to the paddock. Beyond the reach of the lights, he waited in the darkness. He should stay out of this. There was nothing he could do but watch.

There were bright lights outside the tent. At least a half a dozen men in uniform had their guns drawn and pointed at him. He quickly scanned from side to side. There were other people scattered around tents and vehicles. It was dark behind him, no one there.

"Everyone stand still. Anyone moves towards me and this woman dies."

One of the men made the mistake of stepping forward. Without hesitation Jack shot him in the throat. The man gurgled, clutched at his neck, and collapsed like a puppet whose strings had been cut.

"Anyone else moves and they get shot, too."

Jack put the gun next to the woman's head and slowly backed away from the light. Beyond the light it was pitch dark. He kept backing, pulling the woman with him. Now he was ten yards away from the cops. He kept backing up. The men kept still but followed him with their weapons.

He was twenty yards away. He was in the tall grass now and getting close to the edge of the light. Darkness was his ally. They couldn't hit what they couldn't see. He would get away, he had friends and contacts. Get a car and lose himself in a city.

It was slow going in the tall grass and the boot made him clumsy. He was almost clear of the light.

He bumped into something hard behind him. Before he could look there was a blinding pain where his neck joined the shoulder. He screamed. The woman got loose. Then the voice and a gun muzzle in the back of his head. The voice was hard, no hint of doubt, holding itself ready to strike like a coiled rattlesnake.

The man kept backing up toward the paddock, dragging the hostage along with him. Jim stayed down in the grass looking for an opening, some misstep. Then the cops would get him. His palms were sweaty. He gripped the gun tighter. He held his breath and stayed still, afraid any noise would reveal him.

The man kept backing up, getting closer and closer to the paddock fence. Jim tensed, surprised to find himself ready to jump up. Buck stopped eating and was now watching him, too. The man was big . Jim saw a bald head. It was the bald headed killer. He felt a tingle from head to toe. I'm going to stop this bastard. He killed Dave, executed that poor fisherman. I'm not going to let him get away.

Finally the man stepped right against the fence.

With a gleam in his eye and his ears pinned flat, Buck lunged forward and struck, biting the man on the side of the neck.

The man screamed and the hostage broke away.

Jim sprang up and put the barrel of his gun to the back of the man's head and cocked the hammer. He wanted to pull the trigger, needed to. Give me an excuse, you fucker.

The man stiffened when he heard that sound.

"That's right, you bastard. Don't move, not a twitch. Let go of your gun or I'll blow your head off. I killed some of your crew up on the mountain and I'll kill you too. Drop it now."

The man hesitated for a few very long seconds. Jim gritted his teeth, steeling himself to go through with it. A voice in his head spoke to him, urged him on. He tightened his finger, just a few more ounces of pressure on the trigger.

The man dropped his weapon. Half a dozen officers swarmed him and threw him to the ground.

Jim lowered his gun and carefully released the hammer. Without another word, he leaned over the fence and stroked Buck's neck.

"Buck, is this ever going to end?" Then Jim sat down with his back against the fence and shook.

Buck nuzzled his ear and gently exhaled a deep sigh.

Buck nuzzled Jim until Jim finally stopped shaking. Jim turned and stroked Buck's muzzle and breathed into his nose.

Buck went back to munching hay, ignoring the further commotion.

The killer had been handcuffed and roughly stowed in the back of a squad car. People were coming over toward Jim. He waved them away. "We're fine over here, just need some quiet time. Whatever you need from us let it wait 'til morning."

Jim got up and went over to his saddle bags. He fished out his flask of scotch, half full. Jim showed the flask to Buck. Buck snorted and shook his head.

"Okay, fine. Suit yourself. I'm going to drink this down and hope to sleep. You've got your hay and water. Wake me if you need anything."

Jim sat back down near Buck and started sipping the whiskey. He just did not want to think at all. He could see people across from him. Some were staring. He just didn't care.

Chapter 89

His head was throbbing and his mouth felt like a flock of geese had crapped there. He thought, crap, I haven't had a hangover in years. What did I do? Then it all came back to him. The fire, the storm. They'd killed people. They'd got off the mountains. They'd survived. Where is Buck? Then he felt the horse breathe in his face and opened his eyes. Buck was looking down at him, seemed to be smiling.

Jim got up and looked around. The trailhead had cleared out some. There were still tents and squad cars but the fire equipment and ambulances were gone. There was a group of guys in uniform standing by a van.

"Buck, I bet you a nickel they've got coffee and donuts over there. I'll scout it out." And Jim shuffled over to the group.

As he approached, the entire group turned to watch him. When he got closer, he focused on the individual faces. The guys in the blue uniforms, state cops, gave him the steely eye cop stare. There was one guy in brown, a deputy sheriff Jim guessed. Big guy, blond crew cut, early twenties. That guy came forward.

"Howdy, you're Jim, right? The sheriff told me to watch out for you. How are you doing?"

"Feel like I've been in a train wreck, but glad to be down here talking with you. I bet my horse that you guys would have coffee and donuts. Sure hope I win that bet."

The deputy laughed and slapped Jim on the back. "We heard what you did up there. You win your bet." He led Jim to the back of the van and got him coffee and showed him a big box of donuts. Then, the deputy wrinkled his nose and backed away.

Jim laughed. It felt good. "I know. I'm pretty ripe, aren't I? They'll have to hose me off when we get to town."

"Speaking of town, the sheriff is sending someone out with a trailer to fetch you and your horse. A couple of these guys were here last night. They want to give your horse a medal for biting that son of a bitch."

"Ole Buck's not interested in medals, but he'd sure like a donut or two. You guys grab a couple and go on over. He's friendly, only bites criminals."

At that, the whole group chuckled. Several of the cops took donuts over to Buck who soon had powdered sugar on his nose.

"You know that bastard shot one of the state troopers when he tried to escape. The hostage you and your horse saved was a local nurse. Some of us wish he hadn't dropped his gun and you'd blown his brains out."

Jim just nodded his head. He remembered the urge to shoot the guy. A voice in his head had told him to "do it, just do it." He wasn't sure how he'd been able to resist. It frightened him and it wasn't something he wanted to talk about or even think about.

He was nervous around the cops. He'd put on an act, joking about donuts and Buck, to cover his unease. He knew he had some status with them for stopping that bastard last night, but they didn't know yet about what he'd done in the mountains.

He'd left four dead men up there. It had changed him in ways he only dimly sensed. He'd always believed he was essentially a good person, that he was not tinged with evil. But now . . .

"Ah, man." The sheriff and the FBI would have questions. He'd have to rehash the whole ordeal, have to explain each death.

What was he going to say about the men he killed? Time to put on the lawyer hat. The sheriff said he'd been deputized. That would help, even with the FBI. Those bastards would grill him and the numbers... He blew out a breath. Shit, when you look at it that way anybody would wonder if he was a nut case or worse with that body count.

Just keep it simple and matter of fact. Rescuing Bob, protecting the scouts, self defense. Yeah, that would work for the first three. Three! Fucking A, listen to me. I sound like an Elmore Leonard character.

The last guy. I did it out of anger. Can't justify that. Can't explain it, not in a way that the FBI wouldn't pick apart. What to do? Jim looked around, glad no one could read his thoughts, wishing he still smoked. Straightening his back and squaring his shoulders, he made his decision. He hadn't told anyone about the last one. They'd probably find the charred remains, but there would be nothing linking him to what happened to that guy. He would play dumb, plead ignorance. He could live with that, had to. He closed his eyes, blew out a breath.

A few weeks ago he'd been contemplating suicide. He

wondered if his murderous impulse these past few days was some sort of abreaction to that despair. The thought was not comforting. He'd fled here to free himself from all those things that were dragging him down, burying him, smothering his life. And now he had found his true self?

He was rescued from this debate by a squad car racing into the trailhead followed by a familiar truck and horse trailer. The vehicles pulled up in a cloud of dust.

Bob got out of the truck and came over to Jim. Sheriff Thomasen climbed out of the car and joined them. They shook hands, all grins.

"Good to see you made it out, Jim. Guess I'll have to give you and Buck a few days off."

"Darn right you will. The fire was coming right at you. How'd you two get away?"

"That storm slowed us down. By the time we got to the top we could see the smoke. There was nothing we could do but turn around and hope you got away. What about you and Buck?"

"We ran to the reservoir. Had to go through the fire some but Buck kept his head. We'd got pretty wet in the storm which helped. Once we got to the water we were safe."

"You ran through the fire?"

"It was our only choice. Got pretty hot and smoky. Buck was awesome, just put his head down and flew down the trail, fire all around us. What about your camp? Did the fire miss it?"

"Yep, lucked out. It burned itself out against the rock face of Ant Hill. Good thing. All my gear was there and I've got another group of campers coming next week."

The sheriff cleared his throat. "Jim, did you see Stevens at all yesterday?"

"Nope. I saw two bodies by the reservoir. Didn't recognize either one. What about the money?"

"The bald guy, name of Jack Bulganin, had half of it. Our friends the FBI caught the West Slope security chief with the other half. He's got a lot of explaining to do."

Zeke looked hard at Jim. "How are you holding up?"

Jim returned the look and nodded. "I'll live."

"The FBI wants to get the full story from you. They're all paperwork and procedure."

Jim kept his face neutral. "Could you stall them off for a day? I need a shower, clean clothes, hot food, all that stuff." And time to get my story straight.

"Can do. They're still looking for Stevens and one of the kidnappers, the lookout by Ant Hill. Got two choppers up there searching. The FBI is getting a lot of pressure to find Stevens."

"Maybe they're burned up." The lookout sure is, thanks to me.

Zeke shook his head. "I just got a call from our summer clerk. Oscar Savage sold the ATVs the kidnappers used. He finally remembered that the guy who bought them was called Chet."

Bob and Jim looked at each other.

"When you've rested up I want to talk to you about a job, Deputy Taylor."

"Huh. Give me some time." What do I tell the sheriff? Tell him I'm a murderer? Maybe I should just go back up in the mountains, stay away from people.

Bob read Jim's unease. "Zeke, Jim works for me until further notice."

Zeke smiled. "Jim, I'll talk to you tomorrow. Get some rest."

Jim stood there, too tired to think any more.

Bob shook his head. "Are you and Buck ready to go?"

They loaded Buck and drove toward town.

About the Author

Lee R. Atterbury is a trial lawyer in Middleton, WI. He lives with his wife and nine horses. He is working on two other novels featuring Jim Taylor and Buck.

Acknowledgements

This book would never have happened without Sally's constant encouragement. Many others deserve my thanks.

Bob Sundeen for being the best wilderness guide and outfitter.

Jill Wiggen, my long suffering legal assistant, and Alison Heise, who pitched in when Jill was ready to kill me.

Mike Bragg for his patient review of many drafts and excellent suggestions.

Dave Bischoff for early guidance and pointing out great examples.

My readers: Mary Erickson, Betty Erickson, Laurie Hauptli, Megan Landauer, Zay Smith, and Steve Christiansen.

My veterinary mafia: Howard Ketover, DVM, and Michelle Krusing, DVM.

Kim and Greg of Russett Stables for showing me what a reining horse can really do.

Ren Patterson for showing me the way and sending me to BookCrafters.

My children for not laughing at their old man.

And last, Nick, a better horse no man could ask for.